FREEDOM'S CALL

FREEDOM'S CALL

Doug Cornelius

CrossLink Publishing

CrossLink Publishing
1601 Mt. Rushmore Rd, STE 3288
Rapid City, SD 57702

Ordering Information:
Quantity sales. Special discounts are available on quantity purchases by corporations, associations, and others. For details, contact the "Special Sales Department" at the address above.

Freedom's Call/Cornelius —1st ed.

ISBN 978-1-63357-207-2

Library of Congress Control Number: 2019951608

First edition: 10 9 8 7 6 5 4 3 2 1

Dedicated to all those family members, siblings, and friends who were on my prayer team, lifting me up with great love, as I entered the hospital for open heart surgery the spring of 2019.

Level Names - Top to Bottom

Pilot House

Texas Level on Hurricane Deck

Staterooms on Boiler Deck Main

Deck For Freight

Contents

Preface

*F*reedom's Call is based on the true lives of Elijah Lovejoy and African American William Wells Brown, two pre-Civil War champions of the abolitionist movement. The fact that their lives actually intersected briefly made it that much easier to tell their stories and to interconnect their lives with fictional characters, Brady and Charlotte, who must experience those men's daily travails, as well.

Hence, unlike many other historical fiction pieces, Freedom's Call is more than just placing fictional figures into a specific time period. The reader is put right into the decision-making processes of real-life characters whose lives greatly impacted history.

Actual biographies, of course, are excellent resources as well. Hopefully, reading this story will spur additional follow-up by some readers to those tools. *From Fugitive Slave to Free Man: The Autobiographies of William Wells Brown* by William L. Andrews and *Freedom's Champion: Elijah Lovejoy* by Paul Simon were two excellent sources. May this story of intrigue and suspense be your first step in understanding the important roles of these men in our history.

Acknowledgements

T wice monthly I meet with a writers' group held at my church, Church of the Open Door (Maple Grove, MN). Led by Nina Engen and Tim Olson, this group has been extremely valuable to me as I've sorted through various writing issues, striving to continually improve. I also highly regard writers' conferences. Over the past few years, I've attended conferences in Colorado, Florida, and Minnesota.

Many thanks also must go to my fine editor, Deirdre Lockhart.

Chapter 1

St. Louis, MO

Winter 1831

Brady Scott's chest tingled, and a rush of satisfaction welled up into his face. With a direct hit of his snowball, the other boy's black cheek must really be stinging. Feeling the glow of success in his own cheeks, Brady rocked back on his heels and cast a quick glance toward Jamie McKinney. Surely, his leader must have noticed the snowball exploding bright white in the early-morning sun—just his latest bit of expert marksmanship. Barely a teenager, Brady was the youngest gang member, and now, he so wanted to regain the reputation he'd lost in the fury of an earlier battle.

Eyes wide with fear, the struck boy wiped remnants of snow from his dark face and bent to retrieve a box he'd dropped while trying to defend himself. But then the other four boys all closed in, some hurling sticks and stones that also found their mark. Jamie led the way, trying to push the bent-over boy off his feet. But widening his stance, the boy brought his torso back up, plowing his shoulder into Jamie's stomach and bowling him over. The two grappled, fists flying, while the others cheered Jamie on.

* * * * *

Charlotte Jones looked up from her desk as his passing visage eclipsed the window's bright light. A few seconds later, Sandford bolted through the front door, his flailing arms trying to tell a story before words could escape frost-laden lips. She slammed her pencil down. "What's happened to you?"

"Bunch of white brutes," he said, gasping, bending over to catch his breath. "They threw snowballs, sticks, stones—any crying thing they could get their hands on. I was carrying the type from the other printing office." He reached up to feel a scrape on his cheek.

"But why would they?" Such events weren't totally unexpected, especially to the likes of Sandford. She offered him a handkerchief from her pocket.

"Your guess is as good as mine." With the handkerchief pressed to his cheek, he shook his head from side to side and leaned his unsteady body against her wooden desk.

Mr. Lovejoy's office door opened with a bang, its window rattling, and he rushed out to survey Sandford from head to toe. His eyebrows drew together as he bit on his lower lip. "What in the blazes, boy? How'd all this happen? Are you all right?"

"Yeah. But it was scary." Sandford's eyes widened. "Some white boys had me completely surrounded. This big guy tackled me to the ground, and I feared being beat up so bad, my momma wouldn't recognize me no more." He exhaled loudly. "I was able to break loose. Had no choice but to run. I'm a fast runner." An ever-so-slight smile made its first appearance.

"And where's the type?" A new level of concern furrowed Mr. Lovejoy's brow.

"Carried it for a short way, I did, but it was too heavy." As his voice faded, Sandford's smile twisted to a frown. His hands fell to the sides, and a pitiful shrug lifted his scrawny shoulders. "Sorry—had to leave it behind."

"That type's worth a lot." Mr. Lovejoy's mouth flattened. "Hopefully we can still find it if it's not buried in some snowbank. Where did you leave it?"

"In front of the dry goods store." Sandford examined the bloodstained handkerchief.

"I've got to go retrieve it. Charlotte . . . " Mr. Lovejoy turned to her while stroking his stubbled chin. "You're strong for your size. I don't think they'd hurt a girl. Between the two of us, we'll get it back here. Clean yourself up, Sandford, and take the rest of the afternoon off."

Charlotte retrieved her coat and boots. If only she could get her hand past the torn lining into the armhole. A slight tug was all she dare with the frayed bootlaces. Mr. Lovejoy headed back to his office for his outerwear, finishing with a fling of his cashmere scarf around his thick neck. They stepped outside together, the sting of winter's air providing a harsh welcome.

"Who do you suppose those people were that attacked Sandford?" She doubled her steps to catch up with him.

"Probably some teenaged sons of slaveholders." A grimace twisted his face as he focused on the slush at their feet. "Maybe they were feeling particularly entitled today."

She hopped a quick double step as his stride seemed to grow even stronger. "I just can't imagine Sandford doing anything like taunting," she said. "He's such a sweet soul. He wouldn't do anything to get them mad, would he?" She took a gentle swipe at a cloud of her breath as it floated from her mouth.

"I'm not inclined to blame Sandford one bit." He kicked at a mound of snowy slush in his way.

After about ten minutes, they rounded the corner to the dry goods store. Two men were hunched over a box. One looked up. His glaring gaze soon found Mr. Lovejoy's face.

"I know you." He charged forward one step, gritted teeth flashing through twitching lips. "You run that newspaper south side of town. You're probably looking for this." He pointed at the box.

"Must be OK, Charlotte!" Mr. Lovejoy whispered to her, undoubtedly thinking the type was undamaged. He sprinted forward a few steps before his initial reaction of joy faded. He slowed his gait, no doubt not wanting to walk too quickly into the wrath of the rattled man.

Two other strangers stopped at the entry to the store, mumbling something with looks of worry that could not have matched the anxiety she now felt.

"I'm sorry." Mr. Lovejoy squinted. "Do I know you? Your face looks kinda familiar."

"Samuel McKinney. You've got that black boy working for you, right?"

"Sandford, yes. I see you've come across the type he was trying to deliver to my office."

Charlotte stopped in her tracks with a whimper as he approached the box and bent over it.

"Well, that boy hurt my son something terrible. If I ever see him again, I'll whup him till he cries for mercy."

Charlotte's pulse raced. That couldn't be true. She knew Sandford. A pounding in her ears intensified. She so wanted to blurt something out, but words from a half-black girl would never be heard by that man.

"Hold on now, Mr. McKinney." Mr. Lovejoy held up one gloved hand. "Let's just relax. That's not the side of the story I heard. Sandford told me right to my face he was surrounded and outnumbered. All kinds of whatnot was thrown at him, leaving cuts and bruises."

"Rubbish. You're not going to believe the likes of him, are you?" Mr. McKinney stomped his foot, sending a spray of snow over Mr. Lovejoy's precious box—would it hurt it? "He's the one who beat up on my boy." He swiveled his head to the side and spit.

"Then why's this box of type left stranded here?" Mr. Lovejoy lifted both hands now, palms up. "He had to leave it to run to safety."

Mr. McKinney stepped forward, brushing the extended arms aside, his face now mere inches away, his breath fogging into her boss's face. "All I know is my boy was beat up, and this Sandford, as you call him, is going to pay." He pivoted and stomped away.

* * * * *

Several days later, Charlotte sat at her desk finishing her lunch. The strong dill taste of her last crunchy pickle bite was a welcome respite from the smell of ink constantly wafting into the office from the shop.

But then she cringed as Sandford stormed through the door, his head looking almost like a smashed melon, this time much redder than the previous incident. Blood completely saturated his clothes. He breathed heavily as he tried to explain. According to Sandford's account, Mr. McKinney spotted him walking along Main Street, seized him by the collar, and struck him repeatedly about the head with his large cane. As Sandford spoke, blood rushed nonstop from his nose and ears. Her simple handkerchief was not up to the task.

Mr. Lovejoy sent Sandford home to his master. For five weeks, he couldn't walk. When Mr. Lovejoy had to hire a replacement for him, her heart sank to a new low. She'd always felt Sandford a kindred spirit. Like her, he had a white father and a black mother. They had shared how each felt like a pariah to those of the other races. The whites looked down at them as impure. The full blacks were jealous because they did not carry the entire burden of being as black as they were.

And also like her, Sandford was an inquisitive learner. Their two minds would probably never meet up again. And at this point, all she could do was pray for him.

Chapter 2

August 1832

Brady sat at a long table aboard the Tecumseh headed downstream south of Vicksburg, Mississippi. The sidewheeling steamboat was plying the Mississippi River toward New Orleans. Finished with his breakfast, he opened his *Legends of Sleepy Hollow* book and positioned it to capture a shaft of morning sun from the window while his parents dawdled with their breakfast.

"Brady, how can you have your head buried in a book when this is your big day?" his mother asked with eyes as uplifting as her vibrant voice this fine morning.

"Don't worry, Mother. Reading is my diversion to stay relaxed. I'm going to do just fine." He drummed his fingers on the open pages.

His father yanked on a brass chain, and his watch tumbled out of his vest pocket. "Well, you've only got about twenty minutes to get up there. Starts at eight o'clock, right?" With his other hand, he jabbed a fork into his remaining grits.

"The shifts at the wheel are each four hours, and mine starts at eight. If it's like my other stints, the time till noon will go fast."

"Even with Mr. Avery looking over your shoulder at every move you make?"

Brady closed his book. "Father, I've had a lot of practice. This is only the final test to become a cub pilot."

"Well, I still worry about your hearing." His mother spread strawberry preserves on her toast. "There's so much background noise, isn't there?" She pointed the berry-tipped knife his way as her brow wrinkled.

Brady leaned in, tender warmth flooding his chest. "Mother, this is not new. My ears are used to it. Besides, my hearing is much better now—thanks to you." He took a gulping sip of coffee and swiped his mouth with a napkin. "Maybe I'll take a biscuit with me." He grabbed the last one from the basket and pushed his chair from the table.

"We'll be praying for you," she added, her blue eyes sparkling with the excitement of a mother about to see her son lasso his dream.

Brady sauntered to the staircase leading to the texas level where he hoped one day to reside as an officer. He was glad his parents had come aboard for this final test. His mother recognized early on that the prospect of piloting had some sort of spell on him. Now that he was fourteen, she had encouraged him to try out for a spot as a cub pilot last summer. They'd celebrate tonight.

He loved everything about steamboats. Even the sounds invigorated him. From the gentle whoosh of steam behind each stroke of the engine's pistons, to the water lapping off the paddlewheels, to the call of a gull swooping down to check out the river life—he loved it all.

And now as he climbed the steps up to the pilothouse at the very top of the vessel, he noticed a slight tremble to his hands. Had the confidence he displayed to his parents been short-lived? He took in a deep breath, letting the familiar whiff of fresh river air settle his nerves.

Inside, the sun shone through the east-facing side window. Using a rag with his left hand, Pilot Avery was wiping the front window as he gripped the wheel in his right.

"Good morning, Brady. I trust you're up for this. You've got it a bit tougher this time. Water level's down since May. Pilot

Ramsey wasn't feeling well this morning, so it will be just the two of us."

"Yes sir. And I'm fully aware it's completely different going the other way. Making the turns through this winding part will be tricky." He took a firm grip of the wheel.

"Well, you've studied your notes from before, right?" The pilot stepped closer behind him.

"Absolutely." The portly man's heavy breathing warmed Brady's neck, his coffee breath distracting him.

"So, what's the name of the point we're coming up on?"

Brady studied the surrounding trees and shoreline. "Looks to me like Eight Mile Point." He held his chin high, his confidence coming back.

"We'll have to start our turn well in advance. See that huge cottonwood with the big branches hanging over the water?" He pointed ahead off to the starboard side. "When we get abreast of it, start cranking."

Several minutes later, Brady heard the command. "Larboard,[1] son, strong larboard. Lively now . . . lively. Snatch it. Don't dillydally." The pilot's breathing grew heavier.

As he cranked hard left on the wheel, Brady felt a rush when the huge wayward whale at his command responded. But it seemed in slow motion. *When will that tail ever come around? Ah, here she comes. Here she comes.*

"All right now," Pilot Avery said firmly. "You've got to start straightening her out. Come on back starboard with that wheel. Easy now . . . easy. You were a little late with that, but we're OK."

Brady took a quick glance back. Pilot Avery rubbed his bushy eyebrows and lifted his hat, running a hand through his short graying hair.

For the next ten minutes, they had pretty much straight going. A flatboat with cargo passed them going upstream. Brady

---

1 Term used only on the Mississippi to represent toward the left side of the boat.

waved, but no one on the other boat noticed. Or maybe they did but didn't want to wave to someone they didn't recognize. No matter. He felt good—especially after negotiating that last turn. His buddies from his old school days would envy him now. Just about every boy growing up in a river town wanted to pilot a steamboat. Could it be his dream was finally coming true? Would he be accepted as a full-time cub pilot?

Pilot Avery's voice interrupted his reverie. "Remember that long sand point coming up juts out on the starboard side? We've got to go wide around it. Don't be afraid of the cliff to the larboard side. There's plenty of easy water over there—it's deep and clear."

"Yeah, I remember this from my trip upstream last May. Go wide around the sandbar."

"And hug the shoreline. Well, I'm sure you can handle it. But just to be safe, I'm going to be cutting our speed way back." He rang the bell and shouted "stand by" through the speaking tube, his voice carrying down the tube to the engineer. "Pull her back; easy now."

The big boat hunkered down into the water. Its wake quieted.

"Even slower," he followed up, then faced Brady. "I've got to make a trip down to the privy." He gave a wink. "Too much breakfast and coffee this morning. I'll be right back."

Brady turned the wheel larboard to cling closer to the cliff on the left shoreline. This was the first time he'd been given sole control. His hands trembled slightly, so he tightened his grip on the wheel. Soon the sound of the churning paddlewheels reverberated off the cliff.

It got louder. *Seems too loud.*

Had it sounded that way back in May? He must straighten her out—not get too close. As he twisted the wheel clockwise, the stern swung around. He was now heading straight.

Mr. Avery came back, puffing up the steps. "Blazes, what have you done? You're not far enough from the sandbar. I told you to hug the cliff!"

"I thought I was close enough." Brady wiped the moisture from his forehead.

"No, no, no! Not near enough." He rang the bell and called for the sounding team to check the water depth.

With long poles, they rushed forward. Reports soon came back as shouts up to the pilothouse. "Mark three . . . half Twain less . . . Mark Twain!"[2]

"Criminy," said Pilot Avery, huffing.

"We've got no choice. Gotta run it!" He reached for the bells, ringing them loudly. "Full steam ahead. Punch her, boys. Punch her!"

But no response came back through the speaking tube.

"Horsefeathers. What's going on down there? I want everything you've got," he pleaded. "We've got to jump this bar."

The massive vessel seemed oblivious to his commands.

"Seven feet . . . " Brady rubbed his brow. The boat's draft was probably about six feet.

"Get down to that engine room, son. Knock some people on the head. I can't believe this."

Brady flew down the steps past the texas on the third level, past the hurricane deck, to the engine room on the first level. When the boat jerked, he clutched for the railing to retain his balance and cringed at the first sign of the hull catching a ridge.

In the engine room, he sniffed for the robust smell of burning hardwood. Barely there. The boilers only wheezed, hardly more than a sick child. Just before him, the engineer was chastising a young black man, who slammed a book to the deck floor. But with all the noise, Brady could scarcely hear what was being said.

---

2 Commonly used term to represent a mark on the pole equivalent to two fathoms or twelve feet.

"What's going on?" Brady shouted out. "Who's not doing his job down here?"

The engineer jammed his hands on his hips. "When the orders came down, I yelled over instructions to this fella, but he'd disappeared. He's the one who has to get his boys to stoke the furnace. Finally found him in another room. Couldn't believe it—he was reading a book!"

"Well, we had slowed way down." The young black man stared straight ahead, speaking to neither of them. "I thought I could take a break." His words came out low and quiet through gritted teeth. "You want that fire stoked? We'll get her stoked!" He hurried over to the workers with Brady following close behind.

The workers began shoving one log after another into the furnace. The boiler rumbled and hissed. They tossed in more logs.

The boat hull scraped with another jolt on the sandbar.

"It may be too late." Brady reached with a strong tap on the young man's back. "What's your name? I've got to report you to the pilot. And maybe the captain too." He released him to wipe the sweat from his own brow.

The young man hesitated. For the space of a breath, his lips pressed tight. "Name is Sandford, sir. Not too late, sir. We'll get her going."

The boat did gather speed, but soon came another loud scrape and then a forceful jerk. They all caught themselves to keep their balance. The boat ground to a complete halt.

"What? Oh no!" Brady planted a heavy hand on the engineer's shoulder. "Pilot Avery is going to be furious." He pictured him in the pilothouse, slamming his fist down and releasing a volley of cuss words.

Brady searched for what to do next. Then he spotted the book that started the whole mess. He bent over to pick it up and drew his arm back to fling it overboard. *Gotta get rid of this troublemaker.* But it was a copy of *Robinson Crusoe*. He tucked it under his arm.

"Wait, sir," Sandford pleaded. "We can still get her off of this sandbar. Let's go, fellas. I want you to feed that furnace like there's no tomorrow. Give her everything you got!"

"No, no. It's too late," the engineer cried out. "I've been in tough spots like this before. We're stuck. Some tug will have to pull us off."

The young man wouldn't listen, and his workers kept stoking—tossing one log after another into the blazing furnace. The boiler hissed at a higher pitch. The engineer rushed to the pressure gauge where the boilerplates were expanding with a rumble.

Brady headed back up to the pilothouse, escaping the engine room's suffocating heat but knowing Pilot Avery's wrath awaited him. His hot air might be even more suffocating.

Brady jerked the door open inch by inch. Pilot Avery was not manning the wheel. A peek farther around revealed a slumped man on the back bench, his head in his hands. No surprise. After all, they were stuck with no place to go! Brady dared a tentative step in, his ears only half ready for the verbal thrashing.

"What were you thinking, you numbskull?" the pilot lambasted Brady. "We had no business being so close to the sandbar," he said, then kept mumbling it over again. "What did I tell you about the water? It's shallower in July than in May. I told you to hug the cliff. Don't you know what that means? Any knucklehead knows that. No excuses!"

Sucking in a breath, Brady shut his mouth. No point in arguing about what happened in the engine room. He stooped to tuck the book into his satchel.

Then a bone-jarring explosion sent his body flying and his head crashing into the sidewall.

Chapter 3

Brady's woozy head ached. He shook it, trying to regain his senses as hot steam enveloped his body. He shielded his eyes and nose with his forearm and staggered to his feet. Pilot Avery's face emerged from a cloud of steam.

"Are you all right?" He hacked out a cough. "We've got to get below to help people." He put his arm around Brady's shoulder, and they both headed down.

Where are my parents? That was all Brady could think while the blood hammered in his veins.

Before them alongside the texas, on top of the hurricane deck, rested the two smokestacks, now broken and crumpled, no longer proud black spires reaching majestically to the sky. Down one more level, Pilot Avery hurried to the bow toward the men's quarters while Brady rushed aft toward the women's quarters. He shouted out his mother's name, but the chaos drowned his pleas. His stinging eyes made a frantic scan to the water where many passengers were flailing about—some, no doubt, jettisoned by the explosion. *Oh, please, God, help them!*

"Mother!" he yelled, rushing to the aft cabin area. But he soon became hoarse. The heart thumping in his chest had turned into weak thundering in his throat.

Then a terrified man with a scalded face appeared before him. He yanked nonstop on Brady's arm. "Help us! What should we do?"

Brady stopped in his tracks. At the far rear of the boat, a fire had already started. He must think.

"Jump in the water on the starboard side. The water's not so deep over there." He reached to rip wood blinds from the windows. "Here, take these for flotation."

More people surrounded him, imploring for help, but no sign of his parents.

"Pull down more wooden blinds—anything to help you float," he yelled, his voice cracking with emotion. "Six feet—that's not too deep on the starboard side! Gets shallower. The shoreline's not far away."

Dozens of people were jumping into the water from the lower level.

Brady pushed on through the throng. In the main stateroom, people milled about in a daze. Its center chandelier, once stately and glimmering with exquisite beauty, was now just a pile of cut glass on the floor reflecting flashes of light from the nearby fire.

The fire raged most violently in the aft section where deckhands were manning fire buckets. He forged ahead and jumped to the side as an entire wall panel crashed beside him, sending glowing embers flying. Thick black smoke now clogged his breathing. *I thought they'd be back here. Where are they?*

"Mother? Father?" His voice grew weaker as he investigated each cabin still standing. As his voice seemed to be totally spent, he dropped to his knees, his shoulders curling over his chest. Maybe his hopes were giving out as well.

* * * * *

Brady surveyed the throng filing into First Baptist Church, the designated gathering place for the Tecumseh's survivors. The face of the elderly pastor who greeted visitors at the door said it all. Each deep wrinkle of his visage seemed to carry the extra burden of the lives lost. Brady still hadn't found his parents, and as he descended the stairs to the basement where the deceased were laid out, he prayed he'd not find them there.

Then through the blur, he spotted the back of what seemed like a familiar head. Could it be?

"Father!" He pushed ahead of the line, his mouth widening with joy, his heart pounding. But then he saw his father's head disappear. *He must be kneeling.*

His raw hysteria whipsawed—with a stroke of the emotional saw ripping at his knees. His father must be OK, but where was Mother? "No, no." Brady fisted his hands. "Please, Lord, no!" He grabbed the support of his father's shoulder from behind as tears streamed down his cheeks.

His father stood and spun in a daze. When he realized it was Brady, wide-eyed relief commandeered his swollen red face. Large knobby-knuckled hands reached out and grasped Brady, pulling him into the scent of smoke and sweat—a scent that would forever mean loss to him. As tears burned his stinging eyes, Brady returned his father's fierce hug.

"Praise God," his father whispered as they rocked back and forth in each other's grasp. "At least I have you." Then they both turned with anguished faces and kneeled by the side of mother, by the side of wife.

She lay prone on the church basement floor, in a row with what seemed like a dozen other bodies recovered from the steamboat boiler explosion. Her face was pale and expressionless.

"She couldn't swim," his father stammered, his shoulders slumping. "She had to escape the fire, so she jumped in the water but on the deep side." His chest rose and fell with a deep sigh. "That cliff must have looked so close. But alas, I couldn't save her." His chin dropped to his chest. "Oh, my dear sweet Beatrice." He buried his face in his hands. His body trembled, and he continued sobbing.

"Tell me this is all just a bad dream," Brady cried out. But the irony of the situation stared straight back at him. Yes, this dream had begun on a good note when his mother pushed him to try out as a cub pilot. His father's lingering weeping fed the pit of pain in his stomach. This was much more than a good dream gone bad.

"She's gone! I can't believe it. God bless her soul," he whimpered. A refrain his mother had taught him kept echoing in his mind—"Your heart should soar 'cause it's you I adore." That was just one of dozens she called her "'cause it's you" phrases.

"May she rest in peace," his father mumbled. "She was a wonderful woman. I will miss her so."

In the depths of the church basement, Brady felt like they were drowning—no longer from water, but now from suffocating grief. They must seek fresh air.

As they walked together from the church, he looked back at its tall white spire. A cross on top glistened in the late afternoon sun. He had wondered where God was earlier in the day but was sure he was with them now.

Just as quickly, though, that feeling disappeared. No matter how hard he fought it, an overpowering guttural emotion flared up within his chest.

Someone must pay for this. God help me!

Chapter 4

Brady surveilled the two steamboats at the wharf. Two weeks of moping about had passed. Now, he'd seek justice. On the river ahead, a sidewheeler was pointed south, with the last of its passengers stepping on board from the loading gangplank. A tall crate inched along after them, pushed by two young black men, their sweat-glistened torsos shining in the afternoon sun.

This was his opportunity. He hustled ahead and hid behind the crate. As the last boarding whistle blew, he bent and leaned a shoulder into the crate while it crossed the final threshold.

"I'm joining the crew to keep these fellows in line," he said. How ironic that he'd pretend to be the very person he was looking for. He hoped he would find Sandford, whose mismanagement led to the explosion responsible for his mother's death. While searching, he'd stay hidden most of the time since he knew enough about a steamboat's workings.

He crouched between two crates until the steamboat was well underway. The boiler's hissing and rising pitch brought back images of that fateful day. The vision of airborne boards and debris made it seem like yesterday. But where was the person responsible?

Emerging from behind the crates, he sought out the crew tending to the furnace.

"Where's your boss?" he asked the black man carrying a load of cut hardwood to the furnace. But the noise of the wood tumbling from his arms to the deck drowned out his words. Brady asked again, prompting nary a word but a swipe of the sweat from the man's brow, then an arm extended toward a young white man standing with a list in his hand.

"You in charge here?" Brady sauntered over.

"Yeah, what's it to you?" Moving from the list, his darting eyes scanned Brady's rumpled attire before returning to his task.

"Well, I'm looking for a guy named Sandford. Probably has a job like yours."

"I've run into him before. He's not on this boat."

"Any idea what boat I can find him on?" The fellow checked off an item, pausing a moment before looking back up.

"Haven't seen him in quite a while. Last I heard, he was on the Enterprise, but that boat's way ahead of us—probably down by Baton Rouge now. Why? He in some sort of trouble?"

"He was with me on the Tecumseh when it exploded. Saying he's in trouble is a nice way of putting it." Brady's jaw tightened to a grimace as he turned to walk away.

"Wait. I heard all about the Tecumseh. Nobody will take Sandford since that fiasco, if you know what I mean. They tell me he's been hired out to a notorious slave trader named Walker. Sandford helps bring slaves down to New Orleans to be sold."

"So that's what he's doing on the Enterprise?"

"That'd be my guess. Hopefully he's paying attention."

* * * * *

Brady sipped on a cup of hot coffee and leaned back in his chair, breathing in the bacon aroma lingering from the greasy plate on the uncleared table beside him. Daisy's Café was ideally situated along the Natchez waterfront. In a row of shops including hard goods and apothecary stores, it overlooked the wharf and provided an excellent vantage point to monitor the river traffic. The Enterprise was overdue on its return trip upstream. Two scows laden with stacks of hardwood were already tied up along the wharf awaiting the steamboat.

He readjusted the holster of the pistol inside his vest, still uncomfortable with its bulky weight. Weeks had passed since he last fired it while shooting target practice with his father, who had taught him the right way to handle it. He hoped he didn't have to use it, but if need be, justice must be served.

He stood, depositing a couple of coins on the table, and headed out. Sandford's face flashed into his mind. A light-complexioned black man, his curly hair bulged over the sides of his ears, along with bushy sideburns. His peaceful visage bore a stout but not too big nose and not too thin lips, with a slight dimple to his chin. Brady couldn't forget his face.

Eventually, the late afternoon sun on the river's west side shone brightly into his eyes. But two black smokestacks soon appeared above the treetops and eclipsed it. The Enterprise had arrived.

He hurried down to the wharf, arriving as a man called out, "Here now, start that gangplank forward."

A gull circled above, squawking madly. Was it heralding his arrival or portending the future? How had it missed the remains of a fish washed to shore? Even his nose told him that.

The two scows laden with hardwood had already attached themselves to the steamboat's far side. Cut wood was stacked high on each one, towering over the men beginning to unload it. The smell of pine wafting through the air suggested not all the wood was hardwood.

People wearing a myriad of colors traversed the rickety gangplank, bidding their farewell to the Enterprise. Blues, greens, yellows, blacks, and whites flashed by. No sign of Sandford. Brady figured he'd watch every person disembark and then check afterward for those remaining on board.

Once what seemed to be the last of the stragglers made their way off, he rushed on board, yelling to the attendant he was with the wood supplier. A few questions directed to the crew on the main deck were met with shaking heads or blank stares. After about twenty minutes, a man approached the furnace with a stack of wood piled up to eye level. When Brady engaged the eyes, they bulged to the size of walnuts. The stack of cut wood went tumbling to his feet like toothpicks from a spilled box. In the background, the broiler's steady hissing forced his mouth into a sick sneer of remembrance.

The man dashed off.

"Stop," Brady yelled as he tried to pursue but tripped over some of the logs. He positioned his arms underneath him and shoved himself upright just as the dark figure jumped aboard one of the scows, now empty of its load. The man scrambled to untie the securing rope. Grabbing a long pole, he pushed the scow into the current.

Brady grimaced and threw up his arms in disgust as the small raft-like boat was soon moving well downriver. *What to do?*

He grabbed the larboard railing and leaned over toward the other scow, tied directly to where the steamboat's gangplank would rest. It was now almost unloaded, with a young boy helping another man. Brady hurried closer to the man on board, waving to get his attention. "I've got three dollars for you if you'll help me catch the other scow."

"You've got a deal." Brady could hardly hear him as the boy's dog barked nonstop beside him. "I'm responsible for that scow too," the man yelled. "My brother here was poling that one." With a beefy arm, he wiped the sweat from his brow, leaving grimy brown strands of hair stuck to his forehead. "But you help me. We must first finish unloading this last stack."

Brady jumped on board, loaded his arms up, and then deposited the logs by the furnace. The three, with the dog, were soon in hot pursuit of the first scow.

"I only got two poles. You're bigger than my brother. Take this one on the right side."

Brady grabbed the long pole and pushed until striking the soft sandy river bottom. The pole bowed as he muscled it back. Then he lifted and pushed again. Then again. He hoped the young boy wasn't thinking he could do it better. At least Brady could sense they were making good headway as he admired the flowing water that swirled around the pole and glistened in the sun. The other scow was still within sight, and that's what mattered.

"So you know that guy?" the man yelled over. One cheek bulged as he moved a wad of tobacco in his mouth.

"He's responsible for my mother's death." Brady's lips flattened. "I want to bring him in so justice can be served."

"He's angling toward the west shore. Looks like he wants to escape into the woods." The man spit a brown stream of tobacco into the river.

"I don't blame him," Brady responded. "He must feel like a sitting duck in the middle of the river."

The young brother sat petting his dog, now quiet. The boy's face gleamed with the excitement of the chase.

"With the two of us poling, we're catchin' up, but it won't be in time," the man said as he pushed his gray hat down, its brim caught in the brisk wind. "Is he a runaway slave?"

"Suspect so, but not sure," Brady winced with a grimace.

Their scow pulled up to the Louisiana side of the Mississippi about ten minutes behind Sandford. A thought popped into Brady's head, and he rotated slowly to face the boy.

"Say, that dog of yours. Is he the kind that can follow a scent?"

The boy shook his head. "No, Alfie here isn't one of them bloodhounds, if that's what you mean."

Brady frowned, then paid the other man and jumped off, the first step of his boot sliding off a rock into the water. No worries. Wet feet weren't a problem.

Thick woods with heavy underbrush loomed before him. The squawking of a gull high above overlapped the steady washing of the reed-filled shore by the flowing waters. Maybe Sandford was just hunkering down, remaining quiet in the underbrush. Brady drew his pistol. He must leave a message that he meant business. He fired a shot up into the air.

Silence followed the blast. Echoing stillness filled the air. A whippoorwill's weak call finally interrupted the quiet. Brady took a few steps into the dense earthy underbrush, then inhaled a deep breath of the hot sticky air. He leaned over with his hands on his knees. How daunting this task before him would be! He waved at the bugs buzzing around his head. How could he track a strong determined man through the thicket—a man fleeing what he feared was life-threatening danger?

He kicked at the bushy tangle by his feet. This was the deep woods—not the flowing river. It was waiting to swallow the un-suspecting hunter. Today he must not be swallowed.

* * * * *

Sandford's long strides thrashing inland through the under-brush stilled. The shot's blast reverberated in his ears. *Lord, so this is what it's like to be a fugitive slave?* Pushing aside a gauntlet of sumac and pokeberry branches, he pressed on toward a taller stand of cedar trees. With fewer branches clinging to his thighs, he'd make better progress.

Soon he reached a clearing. When his momentum brought him out into the sunlight, his feet skidded. *I must stay out of sight.* He sprinted back toward the comforting cedar shadows, then stopped to catch his breath. Above his own heavy breathing, the trickle of a stream nearby came through. Perhaps following the stream would bring him to another river and lead him to a town. A frog croaking by the steam interrupted his thoughts. Must be telling him to go for it. Hearing no other noise behind him, he took comfort in knowing that, at least for this moment, he'd ren-dered a sense of defeat into his pursuer.

Chapter 5

St. Louis

Charlotte felt like she'd been here before, even though Mr. Lovejoy's office was in a brand-new location. A pile of work papers waited in one corner of his desktop. A larger stack of newspapers occupied another. Elsewhere, a thin film of dust had begun to settle. In the air, a faint scent of ink lingered. But most importantly, the man she so admired sat behind the desk—the man who had returned from divinity school to start up another newspaper.

"I would be most grateful if you could join me here, Charlotte. I so valued your contributions at the *Times*. You are a great person to have around to greet people and do miscellaneous office chores." Elijah Lovejoy leaned back in the chair behind his wooden desk, oblivious to anything on top of it. His bright-eyed face seemed most welcoming today.

"I appreciate your trust in me, sir." With one hand, she massaged the tingle running up the back of her neck. With her other, she brushed some lint from her lap. "But what all will you be writing 'bout with the *Observer*?"

"Religion and morality. My investors think St. Louis needs a new moral voice. I'm anxious to get started."

"Sounds like that might work." She flattened her hands on the beat-up desk before her. The pay would be minimal, but anything these days was most welcome. Pressing her fingertips to the wood's scars, she peered down at her faded blue dress as she rose. A few threads already dangled from a sleeve.

* * * * *

Brady put *Robinson Crusoe* on the bed where he lay as his father entered the room. When he came in with such a serious look, it was time to give him full attention.

"Son, we need to talk." He sat down in a side chair as his hand made a pass at flattening some deep furrows across his forehead. In his other hand, he held a newspaper.

"It's been over a year now since your dear mother died. Now I know you loved her deeply, but you've shown no inclination to get past that accident. You went on a wild chase for the guy—that got you nowhere. Let me tell you, the world has moved on. You've got to stop moping in your room. You gave up on school. Well, our finances are strained. The least you could do is get a job."

Brady bit his lip as a pain welled up in the back of his throat. He sat up on the bed and looked his father straight in the eye. "Father, you know I've tried. But every time I apply for a cub pilot position, I either get rejected or I just never hear back. People are well aware of what happened with the Tecumseh."

"Yes, it's unfortunate." His father rolled the newspaper into a log, frowning at it, his head shaking. Then a deep exhale deflated his chest. "It's fine to hold onto a dream, but there's a point where you have to move on."

Brady crossed his arms in front of his chest, now tightening. He wasn't a sluggard. He must defend his character. "Well, you know, when I have to be one, I'm a hard worker."

"Yes, no doubt. You really worked hard this fall helping me get the crops out of the field. But that's expected—you're a part of this family. Those chores are over with now." His father flicked the newspaper against his knee. "There's an ad in here for a position that might fit you. Apprentice at the *St. Louis Observer.*"

"Apprentice?" Brady gritted his teeth, then spewed out, "I don't know anything about printing."

"Well, it says job duties include proofreading. You always did so well with English in school. And you're a detail person, to boot."

He slammed his hand down on the bed. "Cooped up in an office all day? Father, that's not me. I want adventure."

"You've managed to be cooped up in this bedroom all this time."

Ouch. Brady winced. His old man had a point.

"Sometimes we have to make do. You can always keep your eye out for a cub pilot spot. Your uncle Raymond up in Alton has started supplying wood to the steamboats. He may have some connections. Look into this, please, for me." His father held out the newspaper.

Brady grimaced and snatched the newspaper from his hand.

* * * * *

When a young man came through the door, Charlotte looked up from the box of type she was rearranging in alphabetic order.

"Can I help you?" she asked with a friendly smile.

He stepped forward, brushing his shaggy light-brown hair to the side. His piercing blue eyes met hers. "I'm here about the apprentice job advertised in the paper."

"What is your name?" She set down a handful of letters gently on her desk.

"Brady Scott."

She eased her chair back. "I'll check if Mr. Lovejoy is available." Halfway to his office, she glanced back to see if the young man's blue eyes were following her. They were, indeed.

Once Mr. Lovejoy consented to the interview, she directed Brady to his office. His shirttail hung out from his pants, and mud crusted the heals of his boots. He appeared a bit messy for someone seeking a job. But his wide smile revealing bright white teeth was so enchanting—surely anyone would overlook his outward appearance.

After about twenty minutes, Mr. Lovejoy brought the young man out and introduced him as their new employee. "Brady Scott, meet Charlotte Jones."

"My pleasure," he said. As he extended his arm to shake, his broad shoulders stood out on his otherwise thin, medium height frame. His handshake was firm, his hands a bit rough.

"Brady will be helping out back in the shop setting up the press, but his primary duty will be as a final check on everything written. I gave him a bit of a test in my office, and he came through with flying colors. He'll be starting next Monday." Mr. Lovejoy's tongue darted across his lips.

"It will be nice to have some more help around here." She batted her eyelashes as he said his goodbyes and stepped sprightly out the door.

* * * * *

Sandford took one last look at the harbor, then rubbed his eyes and released a heavy sigh. He was deeply depressed that his owner, Mr. Young, had hired him out to a Mr. Walker, a slave trader transporting slaves to New Orleans for sale. Sandford deemed him a "soul driver," as they were called by fellow slaves.

While in Natchez, Sandford was ordered to watch for the arrival of a connecting steamboat. Since a friend named Lewis worked in a store at the wharf, he headed there. Not finding him inside, Sandford checked the adjoining warehouse. There he found Lewis, his arms tied up high to a beam, dangling with his toes barely touching the floor.

"What's happened to you?" Sandford rushed forward and rested his hand to steady the man's back.

"Oh, Sandford, it's you. This is payback, my friend. I made one last visit to my wife without gettin' the OK." He swallowed hard.

"What? Where is she?"

"Six miles down the road." He gasped for breath. "Sold to someone else."

"And this is what you get for it? Unbelievable!"

"No, there's more. Fifty lashes too." He moaned, and his eyes closed.

A man, who appeared to be Lewis's owner, came into the room. Approaching with a grimace and flaring nostrils, he blurted out, "Just what do you think you're doing here, boy?"

He struck Sandford atop the head with his cane, drawing blood, and instantly, memories of being beat about the head while working as an apprentice for Mr. Lovejoy rushed in.

* * * * *

Headed for New Orleans aboard the Carlton, Sandford struggled to avert his gaze from the Spanish moss along the shoreline. He must instead watch over the suffering humanity behind him. He was responsible for sixteen slaves, both male and female. They were chained two by two on the boat's first level in an area secluded from other passengers. He positioned a stool before one man and instructed him to kneel before him. Sandford opened a straight blade, sat on the stool, and grasped the slave's face to give him a shave.

"This won't do," Sandford remarked when finished. "Boss said if there's still gray whiskers showing, I've got to hide them." He opened a container filled with black pitch-type paste and smeared it over the man's gray stubble. Then wiped him clean with a towel. "There—that's better. Now, how old are you?"

"Best I know, fifty-four." The man rubbed his cheeks. "But maybe you scraped some years off."

Sandford closed his eyes and breathed in slowly as his chest tightened. How could the man have a sense of humor under these conditions? The deep breaths didn't help ease the hurt squeezing at his chest, so he refocused on the man before him. "Boss says if anybody asks, you're forty-two."

"Yes suh." The man nodded.

Once in port, after ensuring all the slaves were dressed properly, Sandford brought them to a pen where prospective buyers could review them. One of the hardest parts for him was encouraging them to look happy.

He raised his arm and yelled out for their attention. "Listen, all of you. If you can sing, I want you to sing nice and loud. Don't worry about how it sounds. Or if you can dance, you must go out and dance. Jump around and look like you're happy, any way you can do it."

Seeing tears in the eyes of those pretending to be something they were not brought tears to Sandford's eyes. He gripped the wire pen so tightly his fingernails dug into his palms.

But the worst part was the heartbreak of seeing them sold to a multitude of interested buyers. Only God knew what sort of life lay ahead for them.

Chapter 6

Brady sat shivering at a desk in the *Observer* office early in January. Ever since the accident, he was always reluctant to throw another log into the stove. His task for the morning was to review copy for the following day's newspaper. An article titled "The Missionary Enterprise" intrigued him.

"So, Charlotte, have you ever been on a mission trip? Elijah has written about it here."

"No, I have not. But someday I hope to." She pushed a file drawer closed.

"This second paragraph seems unclear, though. Here, you read it." He held a paper out toward her. "Tell me what you think."

Charlotte squirmed in her chair and rubbed the back of her neck. "Oh, well . . . I'm not a good one to ask, Brady. I have enough of a challenge keeping the files straight alphabetically."

"No problem. I'll take care of it." He leaned back with his hands behind his head. "So, I never asked you about your Christmas. I hope it was better than mine."

"Spent a nice peaceful one with my mother and auntie at home. What happened at your place?"

"It's not what happened. It's what didn't. It's the second year now without my mother. I miss her more than I can put into words." He tried to direct his thoughts back to the good things about that fateful day—breakfast with both his proud parents, climbing the steps to the sun-drenched pilothouse, his firm grip on the wheel. But then those visions were soon taken over by the horror on peoples' faces, the leaping flames, and bodies floating in the water.

Charlotte interrupted his wandering mind. "You never told me how she died."

"Boiler explosion on a steamboat. This guy kept stoking the fire when the boiler was low on water. Don't know what was going through his head."

"That's sad. So you can't get past it?"

"Nope. I keep getting these little reminders. All the ''cause it's you' sayings of my mom's keep running through my head."

" ''Cause it's you?' What do you mean?" Her head tilted to the side. He so adored the twinkle in her eyes when she was inquisitive.

"Like 'you're sure to inspire 'cause it's you I admire,' " he continued.

Charlotte's eyes narrowed.

"You see it all goes back to some hearing problems I had early on as a young boy. I had trouble distinguishing some words. She'd come up with these phrases with similar words so I would learn to tell them apart. I'd spend hours every week repeating phrases back to her."

"Interesting. So now you're better with your hearing?"

"Much."

"You always seem to listen carefully to what I have to say."

"I try." He bit down on his bottom lip as they pondered in silence.

Charlotte stared over at him until his eyes locked on hers. "Well, any way you look at it, no way a guy should lose his mother as a teenager. I've had to get past not having a father in my life."

"That's got to be just as bad. How old were you?"

"Just a baby. I have no memories of him." Her voice sounded flat and detached. "The sad part is I don't know what I've missed."

* * * * *

Several hours later, Brady found himself watching the grandfather clock up against the office's far wall. Charlotte had disappeared for the last hour, but now as the clock struck four, she came bounding through the door from the shop.

"I'd much rather be doing that than office chores," she said with a smile as she retrieved her coat.

"And what is that?" He gathered up some papers on his desk.

"My sewing. I plant myself at a table at the shop's far corner." She tossed her hair back and put her hat on.

"Sewing?" He buttoned his coat and stepped out together with her into the cold winter air.

"Yes, Mr. Lovejoy has let me set up a table. He's happy to provide the space so I can pursue my sewing on my own time. It's a nice little setup." She nodded her approval.

"I see. Now you're headed home?" He peered out at a most unwelcome slosh-filled road.

"Yes." Her eyes lit up as Brady approached his horse tied to a rail. "I didn't know you had your horse here."

"Well, it's my father's. With the cold, he's letting me save some time getting to work."

"Lucky you." She approached the horse and ran her hand down his long head as Brady mounted. "What's his name?" Her stare focused on the horse's big brown eyes.

"Patches. He's got plenty of blotches of brown and white." He patted the horse's hindquarter.

"What a beautiful-looking animal. Kind of flimsy bridle you've got for him though."

"Yeah, the other one broke. Had to throw this together with some rope." Brady sat quietly in his saddle. "I've an idea. I could help you get home if you like. You could hop up behind me."

She looked down with a heavy sigh and scuffled her shoes in the slush.

"I don't know if that's a good idea. You don't know where I live." She shook her head. "It's way over the east side." A hint of anticipation sparkled in her eyes when she finally lifted her face.

"That's OK. I don't mind. Really," he said with a crisp nod, her dark eyes mesmerizing him. A few seconds ago, they had been transporting her back to her home. Now they gazed up in warm appreciation. Long eyelashes and curly bangs framed them from above, while thin lips widening into a smile with dimpled cheeks framed them from below.

"Well, all right. Let's give it a try," she said, and he reached for her hand as she put one foot in the stirrup, then swung her up behind him.

"There we go." He savored the warm embrace of her arms wrapped around his waist. They headed out, forging ahead through a January cold that now didn't seem so bad.

As they clopped along, he felt fortunate to be riding so high, hardly noticing some slushy snow down below. Charlotte pointed the way. With his flimsy rope bridle, he had to double his efforts with the reins. After an extended period of quiet, he asked, "So, what is it with all the sewing?"

"Oh, that's something I've always had an interest in. Mama has taught me. As long as I can remember, I've wanted to become a seamstress."

"It's great Mr. Lovejoy has let you set up a table in back. Sure wish I had a way to keep chasing my dream."

"And what is that?" She pressed her head around to the side, her cheek touching his, making for a warm tingling.

"Well, I can tell you it's not proofreading articles and setting up presses." He gave Patches a healthy kick.

"What is it, then?" She squeezed her arms tighter around his waist.

"I want to be a pilot on a steamboat. I've been a cub pilot off and on for over a year. Just waiting for another opportunity."

"You mean if the chance came up, you'd drop everything?"

"In a second." He pictured himself cranking the wheel full starboard, the stern of the boat swinging around just as he had planned.

But his reverie soon turned to reality. Buildings near them now stood in stark disrepair. Roofs were missing shingles, their facades revealing splintered wood crying out for paint. Broken steps no doubt made visitors feel most unwelcome.

"I'm just another block farther down," Charlotte said. "My mama should be home from work by now. You're welcome to come in and meet her."

"N-no, that's all right. S-some other time," he stuttered. "My father's probably wondering where I'm at."

* * * * *

When Charlotte entered the office the following morning, she found Brady already there reading a book.

"Good morning," she said, then waited for him to lift his head.

"Yes, indeed. It is a fine morning." His eyes glistened as he pushed a bookmark into place and closed the book cover. "I brought something for you." He held the book up. "I thought maybe we could read it together." His probing eyes landed squarely on hers.

"Oh, really?" She hoped her voice didn't sound too anxious. But her shoulders slumped as she pressed her lips tight.

"It's something I really need to work on. I know that." Her heart skipped a beat. Inwardly, she rejoiced in knowing her well-being was important to Brady. She hung her coat up on a pole and returned to look at the book. She opened Robinson Crusoe slowly, the spine crackling a bit beneath her touch, and felt a hollowness in her chest. So many of the words were unrecognizable.

"I don't know, Brady." She sighed heavily, then took a deep breath trying to fill that hollow spot. "I appreciate you want to help me. But just when will we have time for this?"

"Before our start here, early each morning. I could pick you up with my horse each day and bring you back home after work."

"Well, if I have any extra time, I'd rather be sewing in the back." She rubbed her forearms.

"Couldn't that wait? Save that for afternoons after work. Do both!" His dimple appeared.

Still frowning, she let the book close on those scarily big words and turned her gaze to his kind face. "So you'd make extra time both before and after work? Just for me?"

"Yes, not a problem." He leaned in with a gleam in his eye.

How dear he was! A strange warmth heated her cheeks. "That's generous of you. But I wish I felt better about the reading."

"That's exactly why we need to do it. Plus, it's a wonderful story you'll enjoy."

Chapter 7

As the wintry months of January and February dragged on, Charlotte felt blessed indeed to have Brady offer her horseback rides to and from work. They often used their time together to talk about the story the author Daniel Defoe laid out in Robinson Crusoe. Her reading improved. When she asked Brady about certain words, he usually knew their meanings. Other times, they talked about current happenings in the community.

"I sure am glad my mama and auntie can teach me about the Bible," she said as the rising sun warmed them one Monday morning. "They've been trying to set up a Sunday Bible school for a number of young people at our church, but they've run into nothing but grief."

"How's that?" Brady prompted his horse with a kick to speed up his gait.

"My friend, Malcolm, his brother, and all of their friends—they're still slaves—not freed like me and mama."

"They're still coming to church, right?" With the road now more slush-filled, the pleasing clip-clop of hooves was more like slip-slop.

"Oh yes. But some have been fighting against teaching them 'bout the Bible. We heard there was even an editorial in Mr. Lovejoy's old newspaper, the Times, saying slaves shouldn't be taught religion."

"Really?" Brady tipped his head back, a frown pinching his lips tight and furrowing his brow. "I'll bet Mr. Lovejoy wouldn't be happy to hear that. You should tell him. He'd probably come back with an editorial of his own in the Observer."

Later that day, when Charlotte discussed it with Mr. Lovejoy, he said he thought denying religious freedom was monstrous and horrible. He went on to say the paper's attitude was shameful.

"But you're not for abolishing slavery altogether?" She had to ask for clarification.

"No, the country isn't ready for that yet." Mr. Lovejoy stabbed a pointer finger against his desk to emphasize his words. "But they have souls as precious as those of their master."

"I feel so sorry for Malcolm," Charlotte told Brady on their way home from work. "He so wants to learn."

"Maybe that's where you'll have to step in, Char." Brady twisted slightly in the saddle to look back at her. "Who is this Malcolm, anyway? You'll have to introduce me." He released an uneasy chuckle.

"He's been a dear friend. We've practically grown up together. He works as a tanner in his master's livery stable farther east by the river."

"I see. Maybe he could make me a new bridle? This rope one is about to fall apart." Brady held up the reins and shook his head.

"He'll do just about anything for me if I ask him. He's just a very special guy."

* * * * *

Winter's dreary cloud-covered days passed slowly. As spring approached and the sun warmed the air for more hours, peoples' spirits rose as well. Before the workday was to begin, Charlotte sat in the printing office reading *Robinson Crusoe* while Brady organized some papers to review.

"I've got some bad news." His low voice broke the silence and blunted her spirit.

She placed her finger on the word she'd just read and gave a half-chuckle. "You'd better break it to me, but be gentle."

"Nothing serious. Father just told me he needs the horse to help plant the crops. I won't be able to pick you up anymore."

"Oh well—that's not the end of the world. It does mean, though, more time walking and less time reading."

Brady stood up and stepped toward her, his eyes appearing to search for her spot in the book.

"Are you enjoying the book?" His upturned face seemed to beg for a positive response.

"Yes, but I must admit, some of the words are still a challenge." She shuffled her feet, scraping the soles of her shoes on the gritty floor. "I find it interesting that Robinson Crusoe is now a slave in the story. We'll see how he likes it."

"Slavery is indeed a part of the story. It was certainly well entrenched back almost two hundred years ago."

Charlotte remained quiet a moment, her finger pressing so hard against the page it bent backward painfully. She loosened the tension in her touch and released a long breath. "So does your father need you to help him plant the crops?"

"Yes, I'm going to have to ask Mr. Lovejoy for some time off." He bit his bottom lip.

"I overheard him talking about the poor state of our finances. Sounds like that wouldn't be a problem." She thumbed through the book's front pages. "Say, did you ever notice the note at the beginning?"

"Yeah, the one to a William? I hold him responsible for my mother's death." He averted his gaze. "I've felt like ripping the page right out."

"But it's part of this book's story, isn't it? Books take on their own stories depending on who has read them and how it has impacted their lives."

Brady sat quietly. "You've got a point. I tell you, Charlotte, you may not be well educated, but you're perceptive well beyond your years. Since you're taking all that into consideration, I just wish this book had a better story behind it."

"What do you make of the person who signed it? Parish L." Her brow furrowed.

"Can't tell you anything about it." He shrugged.

* * * * *

Sandford knew his mother was on the boat docked in front of him—one destined for New Orleans, so why wasn't he rushing on board? Wouldn't each moment with her be ever so precious? He also knew those moments might be his last. Facing that reality wrenched his heart. *Will I ever see her again?*

He was drowning in guilt. In an ill-fated dash for freedom, he had tried to bring his mama with him in his last escape attempt. Yes, she slowed him down, but he couldn't leave her behind. And now both were recaptured, with different masters, and their fates would bring far-reaching separation. He would stay near, as a steamboat steward. She would go far, as a fieldworker on a distant plantation in the Deep South.

He finally approached her as she remained chained on the boat, one of many about to sail for New Orleans.

"I blame myself, Mama, for all this. Trying to escape was my idea." He lowered his head close to hers, his eyebrows pinching together. As her downcast face rose to meet his and her lips flattened, a slight whimper of anguish came from deep within. It was multiplied a thousand times over in his own heart. Her shoulders now jerked as she tried to raise her hands, but sadly, they were bound tight.

"I know, Mama, you'd caress my cheeks if you could, just like when I was a little one. I am so, so sorry it all ended up this way." He lightly stroked her wet face with two large fingers, dwarfing her sullen cheek.

"My dear son. You are not to blame for my being here. You have done nothing more nor less than your duty. Do not, I pray you, weep for me. I cannot last long upon a cotton plantation. I feel my heavenly Master will soon call me home, and then I shall be out of the slaveholders' hands."

She looked up, creases forming across her forehead as her owner approached. She whispered into Sandford's ear. "My child, we must soon part to meet no more this side of the grave. You have always said that you would not die a slave—that you would be a free man. Now try to get your liberty! You will soon have none to look after but yourself."

Her owner came up to Sandford and kicked him with his boot. "Leave this instant!" he shouted.

As Sandford left, his mother gave one last shriek. "God be with you!"

The words echoed in his head.

* * * * *

On a Sunday afternoon in April, along the shores of the Mississippi just south of St. Louis, Charlotte pranced ahead of Brady. She dipped her hand into the flowing river. "Brr . . . it's still ice cold. The bright sun lulls you into thinking it'd be warmer."

"Well, I dare you to take your shoes off and wade in," he replied as he strolled along, the reins of their horse in his hand, walking behind. With his other hand, he flung a stone out skipping along the water's surface.

"No way, I'm not taking your challenge." She pinched her shoulders together.

Brady pulled the horse ahead. "We're just about to the spot. See that big rock along the shoreline? That's where I'd sit and watch the steamboats go by after school—that's if I had all my chores done."

"When was all that?"

"Oh, it all started when I was about ten."

"Then let's stop and see what goes by. I'll break out the crackers and cheese." She steadied Patches and reached for the satchel draped over the saddle horn.

As they sat on a blanket draping the rock, a barge loaded with cut wood passed before them, heading slowly north against the strong current.

"You'd leave your job with Mr. Lovejoy to work on one of those?" She nipped a corner of her cracker.

"Not a barge. But yes, I'd leave in a flash to work as a cub pilot on a steamboat. That's if somebody would have me." He grabbed a nearby stick.

"That explosion incident still haunts you?"

"It always comes up when I'm asked about my experience." He snapped the stick in two. "Well, at least I have my uncle with his ears tuned to any mention of an opening. He sells wood to the steamboat operators."

A sternwheeler came around the bend heading downstream.

"Wow!" Brady exclaimed. "Look at that beauty glide along so effortlessly. Those smokestacks, don't they look magnificent with their billowy smoke drifting away? What I would give to be piloting her. Although, truth be told," he snickered, "I'd prefer a sidewheeler—they're more maneuverable."

"Seems like it would be fun at first." She crumbled a bit of cheese atop a cracker and closed another over it. "But wouldn't it get routine?"

"You've got to have a heart for adventure. Around every bend is a new vista. Seems around every bend there's a new story too. Sometimes I feel like the river is actually talking to me. One time, it will be the voice of some pilot I've worked with. Another time, it's the birds squawking, telling their story. I can't help but think about the river's soul—how it is ever-changing. The water never stays the same—it's always new, even though all the outward landmarks may be the same."

"It's kind of like with new water comes new opportunities, right?" She gazed out into the distance.

"You bet." He put his arm around her shoulder and felt a rush as he pulled her tight. No doubt, Charlotte was starting to capture his heart. She was so charming, with an even-tempered personality. She was curious, willing to learn, yet already so perceptive. He turned to explore her piercing dark eyes. In the bright sun, they were especially alluring beacons on an undoubtedly beautiful face.

A young couple strolled by dressed in their best Sunday attire. The man held a small umbrella over his lady, shielding her face from the sun's bright rays. He looked toward Brady and Charlotte together, releasing a mocking, shaming whistle while shaking his head. After a few more strides of staring, the lady cried out with a scolding voice, "How inappropriate!"

As if chiding from adults wasn't enough, some small sticks began to descend from the sky, striking them on the tops of their heads. The sticks' source was not readily apparent, but Brady soon determined they came from behind a nearby lilac bush, showing its spring buds.

"This has got to stop," he demanded while jumping up from the rock they'd been resting on. He ran over behind the bush and gave chase as two young boys took off giggling. His legs, however, feeling heavy, were too accustomed to desk duty and unworthy of the challenge.

Chapter 8

Cody Cuthbert's ma slammed the kitchen cupboard door, rattling its splintered frame.

"Don't you take that chicken yet, Jeb Cuthbert," she warned his pa as she scurried to the stove, a scowl on her face. "It's still half raw," she bellowed with her nose turned up.

"Enough of yer fussin', Sally. It'll be fine for the dogs. I'm in a hurry. You took too long pluckin' them feathers. Long as we can pull the meat off the bones. Now drain off that water so we can get at the meat."

Ma poured off water into the rust-crusted steel sink, then got a plate from the cupboard. She plopped the carcass on the plate and tried to pull off strips of meat. When that didn't work, she grabbed a knife.

"You realize we gotta make dinner out of this too? Never heard of dogs getting fed before people," she muttered while shaking her head. She shoved the plate with meat on it at pa, who right off headed outside. He returned with a small pail in his hand, the plate covering its top.

Cody strode over to look under the plate. "Glad you're not feeding that to me," he said while making a choking noise in his throat.

"Zeke and Buddy, they'll love it." Pa shoved a wad of tobacco into his mouth. "They don't care how pink it is. You heard yer ma. She can cook what's left some more." He grabbed two leashes from a nail in the wall, and Cody followed him out the door.

"Do you reckon Buddy's going to be a fast learner, Pa?" Cody grabbed for the pail's handle.

"I 'spect so. If he's half as good as Zeke was, he'll have earned his keep. Zeke, for a bloodhound, he's getting purty old. Who knows, he may just sit this one out."

A few steps from the door, they were greeted by the two dogs, tails wagging and mouths yapping. Not even a late afternoon May sun could brighten up Zeke's gray hair, in contrast to Buddy's reddish brown.

"Pay attention now, Cody. Guard that pail. Don't let them get their snoots in there." Pa attached the dogs' leashes. "Now take off your shoes and give me the socks."

"I only got one sock on, Pa."

"All right—just give me that one, then. Now, I'm goin' to start out with Zeke to show Buddy how a good dog does it. Gotta be able to chase down them runaway slaves." He leaned his head back with a smile and sang out, "Fetch, find, found. I'm a lovin' my hounds," while shoving Cody's sock into Zeke's nose.

"I'm holdin' the dogs here, Cody, while you take the pail with you. Go hide way over yonder past the wheelbarrow behind them pine trees. When Zeke finds you, I want you to give him a nice piece a chicken for a reward. Got it?" He spit out the side of his mouth as if there were no two ways about it.

Barefoot Cody trudged with the pail toward the trees. Passing the wheelbarrow leaning on its side, he gazed down at the broken wheel sitting crooked on its axle. Had been like that for over a year.

After a few minutes, he heard his pa cry out, "You all set? I'm sendin' him."

Moments later Zeke was pushing his nose into Cody's hand. Cody reached into the bucket for a couple of choice pieces of chicken. Zeke gulped them down in seconds, and then pa called Zeke back.

"OK, right quick I'm goin' to send Buddy."

But Cody waited longer than expected.

"No, not that squirrel! Go see Cody! Go see Cody!" came his pa's yell. While waiting, Cody peered into the bucket. His nine-year-old's curiosity was not to be denied. He soon had both hands deep into the chicken, comparing the texture of the still-pink white versus dark meats.

Buddy finally came charging around the corner of the pine trees and found Cody. He clamped down on both the chicken and Cody's hand.

"Aaargh!" Cody screamed out. "Pa, he's got my hand and won't let go. Help! Pa . . . help!"

His pa came running. "Can't you get nothin' right, boy?" he said while trying to pry Buddy's jaws loose from Cody's hand. "What did you do? Tease him with it?" he muttered, a scowl darkening his face and pulling down his bushy eyebrows.

"No, Pa. I didn't do nothin'." Cody held his hurting hand up with the other, looking at a small wound.

"We've got some work to do with this one yet." Pa pointed to Buddy. With his boot, he took a half-hearted swipe at the dog's ribcage, then scowled at Cody. "What's a'matter with your hand? Don't be fussin' over a tiny spot of yer blood." Pa grabbed the pail. Cody trotted after him, with Buddy by his side sniffing his hand as they walked back toward the house. Pa was in a different world, chanting, "Fetch, find, found. I'm a lovin' my hounds."

* * * * *

As the year 1833 wound to a close, God put Brady on the steamboat Chester on the Ohio River. It had Brady pinching himself. He now had the opportunity to corner Enoch Price, owner and captain of the boat, about a cub pilot job. True, Elijah Lovejoy had sent him to Cincinnati to listen to an abolitionist named Theodore Weld, but that job opportunity wasn't what had his blood pumping on this chilly afternoon.

"Who are you?" came the gruff greeting after Brady knocked on a door in the officers' quarters later that afternoon. The man continued to button his dressy shirt.

"Brady Scott, sir. I'm sorry to bother you, Captain Price, sir, but I was inquiring about a cub pilot position."

"How'd you find me?" His eyes narrowed and squinted.

"Well, my experience has made me quite aware of the layout of exquisite vessels such as this, sir."

"Is that so?" A smile formed on Mr. Price's round and ruddy face. "My pilot did say something about a possible spot a couple weeks ago." He paused in thought while he worked to insert a cufflink in his sleeve cuff, perhaps in preparation for a night on the town. He looked Brady up and down. "I like your determination. We're in port another day, so meet me here tomorrow afternoon at 3:00 p.m. sharp. We'll sit down with Pilot Jenkins."

"On New Year's Day, sir?"

"Yes, that's fine. I expect Jenkins will have a clear head by then." He turned with a chuckle and closed his door.

* * * * *

At the appointed time the following day, Brady sat with both gentlemen in the captain's stateroom. Brady put a hand down to steady his twitching knee. He felt cramped with the three of them all together in a small, albeit well-kept, room. Mr. Price's husky frame overshadowed his tiny metal desk as he sat behind it.

"So, you were saying, Brady," the pilot inquired while leaning back in his chair, "you've plied the waters of the lower Mississippi. Tell me, on the first major bend north of Natchez, what's the unusual thing a pilot needs to watch for?"

"Well, there's a sandbar, sir, that seems to disappear, but then when you least expect it, there it is again."

A knock on the cabin door interrupted them. A black steward holding a tray with hot tea entered, a white serving cloth draped over his arm. Dressed in dark pants with a server's vest, he poured three cups of tea and walked back to the door to depart. Brady did not get a direct view of his face, but his sideburns appeared vaguely familiar.

"Thank you, that will be all," the captain said to the steward. "There are many passengers disembarking today, so please help them with their luggage."

"Yes sir," the steward responded, closing the door behind him.

For the next half hour, Jenkins quizzed Brady about his experiences and knowledge of the Mississippi River. Captain Price returned to his desk, seemingly to attend to other matters. Jenkins was leaning back in his chair with a contented smile when someone banged on the door and burst right in.

"Captain!" a man blurted out with shortened breath. "You won't believe this. Sandford has taken off. I saw him lug some passenger's big trunk on shore. Then, in the midst of the crowd, he just turned and took off for the woods. He didn't come back."

"What? I can't believe it! Seemed to be a good man. I just bought him last October." He cast his eyes down, his head shaking. "We always take a risk when we come to free territory, but I sure didn't expect Sandford to take off."

"Sandford, you say?" Brady almost leapt from his chair. "I thought he looked familiar. I was a cub pilot on the Tecumseh with him. Got grounded on a sandbar. He stoked the fire, and it blew up. My mother was just one of many who died . . . " His voice trailed off.

"Oh . . . " Jenkins jaw dropped, and the room became dead silent as Brady's shoulders slumped.

What have I done? Brady closed his eyes, wincing his defeat. *Blurting out all those details! What must be going through their minds now?* An overwhelming heaviness pushed him even farther down into his chair. He rubbed his temples while closing his teary eyes. Deep within, his chest trembled. Tales of being black-listed were no longer just tales—they were coming true. Then the conversation swirling around him came back into focus.

"I must get this man back." The captain slammed his fist on his desk. "Who has any ideas?"

"You need to send somebody after him, sir," Jenkins said.

"A bounty hunter?"

"I'm afraid so. It will cost you some money, depending on what you think he's worth to you."

As if reminded he was still there, the captain waved a hand. "Oh, Brady. This new matter has come up. We have some other candidates we're considering. That will be all for today."

Brady had sunk so low in his chair, he felt glued to it. He couldn't move. Images of that fateful day filled his head—suffocating steam, burning staterooms, and fleeting, fear-struck faces. Worst of all, his mother's rigid body lying on a cold church basement floor. He couldn't say a thing—anger choked his throat. Now there was no doubt. Sandford had cost him in two ways—not only was his mother gone, but also his dreams of piloting a steamboat were gone as well.

Seemingly oblivious that Brady had not yet departed, the captain continued, "I'm willing to pay good money just to get him back. Do you know someone in this business, Jenkins?"

"There's a man right here in Cincinnati with a reputation—Cuthbert I think his name is." As the bearer of this relevant information, Jenkins seemed to be bouncing on his toes. "He uses bloodhounds. We'll have to find something with Sandford's scent." His eyes scanned the room. "His serving towel over there should work. Do you want me to try to locate Cuthbert?"

"I assume that means he brings him back alive, right?" The captain's lips pressed together in a slight grimace.

"That's always the plan going in." Jenkins wrinkled his nose. "But you are aware, Captain, according to, I believe Section 32 of the law, if he resists capture with a counterassault, it's legal to kill him."

"Heaven forbid. I hope that doesn't happen." He shook his head and looked to the ceiling. "Anyway," he resumed, "I've got one hundred seventy-five I'm willing to pay. Go find that Cuthbert guy who's got the bloodhounds."

"Make that two hundred," Brady piped in. "I've got twenty-five to add to the pot."

Chapter 9

The following evening, Brady sat in a daze in the back row of the church whose name he had already forgotten. This is why he had come to Ohio. Mr. Lovejoy wanted him to hear Theodore Weld lecture, so the Observer could feature him in an article. Weld traveled farther west than any other champions of the day promoting abolition.

Brady tried hard to push out flashes from the previous day—how had he actually been in the same room as the man whose deeds he felt compelled to avenge. Sandford, now a fugitive slave.

Before him at the lectern stood a man in simple attire, but with a powerful voice. Claiming he had a direct responsibility to God rather than some church or organization, Weld noted he felt most comfortable in his "John the Baptist" attire.

He spoke of mounting stories of the maltreatment and deaths of slaves. One such story involved a slave in New Orleans accused of stealing meat who was driven into a harbor by a mob and ended up drowning. Other stories depicted the sale and separation of children from their mothers.

But more than the cruelty and maltreatment, Weld was concerned about their freedom. Slavery destroyed their humanity—he even called it a "death stab" to their souls.

For the entire evening, Weld's flowing oratory soared. Some in the audience thrust their fists to the sky, their cheeks shining. Brady felt his own pulse jump. But others jeered with clenched jaws, their angry eyes bulging with disapproval.

* * * * *

A day later, hunkering deep in the woods by some sumac bushes, Sandford munched on several crackers he'd brought. He thought well of himself for having at the last minute carried along some provisions, as well as a tinderbox for making fires. But when icy shudders persisted in running up his spine, he regretted not bringing an overcoat.

A thin veil of snow covered most of the trees and their branches but melted underfoot, leaving slippery mud. And since the sun had long set and darkness enveloped him, he felt confident in heading out. Tonight the sky was quite clear. Finding the North Star shouldn't be a problem. He followed a path and cautiously stepped onto the main road. His eyes on the sky, he soon found the bright star that would lead him to Cleveland. From there, perhaps Buffalo. Then Canada and freedom. Sandford repeated the word out loud. Who cared if he was a fugitive slave? He was on his own on a journey to freedom. *Hallelujah!*

The clatter of a horse-drawn carriage approaching from behind startled him. He hurried to the cover of the woods. *Dare not risk meeting anyone, much less talking to them.* As he crouched, the wind carried a wolf's distant howl. At least it sounded like a wolf.

The carriage passed, and when it was well beyond the view provided by the half moon, he resumed his journey. And so he continued mile after mile, often blowing in his hands to warm them. When he slipped on the icy surface of the hard-packed roadway, the energy exerted regaining his balance helped him feel warmer.

After what he figured must be over a dozen miles, he came across a farm not far from the road. The dim early morning light revealed a barn bleached gray from years of exposure. Behind it, farther back on a hill stood a two-story clapboard-sided house facing a stretch of road to the south.

With the morning about to break, he'd best find shelter again rather than brave the daily activity of a gaggle of folks whose trustworthiness was unknown. Hopefully, he could spend the daytime hours sleeping in the barn's upper loft, the soft hay providing a pleasant respite from the poking of sharp branches in the woods.

He creaked open the back door, and the smell of a place where barnyard animals called home was welcoming. But a familiar odor was not enough to make him comfortable. He was still a trespasser in someone else's barn. How often had black trespassers been shot without question? His thoughts were interrupted by a woman coming around the corner with a lantern in one hand, a rifle in the other.

"What you doing, mister?" Her voice, stern and unwavering, carried in the clear morning air.

"Oh, you startled me, ma'am! I-I mean no harm. I was just hoping to find a quiet place to sleep." He peered down at the short woman. The lantern light shone upon her heavily wrinkled face with sunken cheeks and highlighted the frizz around gray hair pulled back and tied.

"Well, breaking in ain't the way to do it, boy. Where you from?"

"Cincy. I'm on my way to see my sister in Cleveland."

Hoisting the lantern higher, she scanned him from head to foot. "Fancy pants and a vest?" A sneer spread across her face. "Don't see them on the likes of a person of your sort."

"Oh yes. I work as a steward on a steamboat. No time to change before I left. My sister came down sick real sudden."

"Well, you seem to talk OK." She paused. "I s'pose yer hungry too. I got some leftover oatmeal in the kitchen if you want it."

"Yes, I'm very hungry. Much obliged." Sandford felt uneasy about the strange woman, but like a puppy obeying its master, he followed her to the kitchen. Dim morning light from a small frosted window did little to brighten up the large space.

"Set yerself down there." She pointed to a square wooden table with four chairs. She put the rifle down only long enough to dish up some mush from a pot on the stove. The old lady deposited the bowl with a spoon and napkin on the table. She looked back at another plate on the counter. "Well, ain't you a lucky son of a gun this morning. Just happen to have a leftover sausage looking pretty lonely over there on the counter." She moved the plate to the table. "Coffee?"

"Yes ma'am. I'd love a cup. Thank you."

As she poured the coffee, she said, "I have to go upstairs a minute. I'm going to trust you to stay in your seat and not move. Ya know, these ears of mine can still hear real good. They can pick up the slightest screech of a chair. Don't even think about movin' that chair out, not even an inch. Got that?"

She grabbed both the lantern and rifle and headed upstairs. Sandford stared at the sausage. Cravings from his stomach growled loud and long. But no, he'd need something later. He wrapped it in the napkin and tucked it in his pocket. He leaned back, feeling safe from the winter winds, whose shrill shrieking through the window cracks would rise and then fall silent. Then the footfall of the lady's imminent return startled him.

"Where's your husband?" he blurted out as she stepped back into the kitchen.

"None of your business," came her steely reply as she gripped the rifle tighter. Sandford's eyes escaped the penetration of hers by focusing on the few remaining bites in his bowl.

"That were good, weren't it? I do pride myself on my cookin'." The first smile he'd seen from her flashed across her face. "More coffee?"

She retrieved the pot as well as a cup for herself. As she poured, she asked, "So, what boat you been a steward on?" Then she sat in a chair across from him, cup of coffee in hand.

"The Chester out of New Orleans."

"That a sidewheeler?"

"Yes ma'am."

"My husband and I took a boat to N'Orleans once—seems like ages ago. I think it was called the Tecumseh."

Sandford's face froze.

"I know that boat. I once worked it," he confessed. His head shook back and forth in regretful musing.

"Bet your time was special."

Sandford remained quiet.

She swirled the coffee in her cup, gripping the pink and white china in both hands. "Being a steward . . . that must be purty easy."

"To be honest, some days I feel like I'm just some fellow Friday working for Robinson Crusoe."

"Some what?"

"Never mind." He stared vacantly off into the distance.

"Easier than workin' the fields, right?" She took a big swig of coffee.

"You bet. I've done both." Images of his mother and sister flashed into his head. "Yeah, that's what I fear my mama and sister are doing right now—way down South somewhere."

"Bet they work hard as any man." She slowly eased back her chair, as if foreshadowing a new topic. "What else you done?"

"Well, I've prepared other slaves and herded them into pens at the ports to be sold."

"Other slaves?" She paused. "That's kinda strange." A smirk twisted those wrinkles across her face. "A slave herding other slaves? Interesting—"

"What?" Sandford jerked his head up, exploring her eyes.

"Yer one of them what they call fugitive slaves, ain't you?"

Sandford fidgeted and dropped his spoon, but didn't answer.

"I knowed it!"

His face froze in a grimace as he pushed his chair hard from the table with a screech he was sure was louder than any the woman ever heard. But then came quiet. In the distance, barking of dogs punctuated the thick silence. Sandford leapt to his feet, anger choking his throat as coffee spilled all over the table.

"Yer the second one this month I seen pass through," she crowed with a whine.

He lunged toward the door.

"No sense rushing out. Cuthbert will be here right quick. Me and guns don't work so good together, but me and him do." A smile crinkled her face. "He knows to make a beeline for the house when I put a lantern in the window upstairs."

Sandford bolted into the cold mist of the early January morning. Behind him, the old lady stood in the doorway yelling, "Fetch, find, found. He's a lovin' his hounds."

Shivering seized his body. Was it from the cold or the yowling of her voice that howled as bad as the dogs?

Chapter 10

Having returned to the *Observer* office, Brady sat with Mr. Lovejoy and Char, telling them about Theodore Weld's lecture. With animated arms, he punctuated his description of the abolitionist's talk. "For such a simple-looking man, he sure had soaring oratory filled with passion."

"I expect you took copious notes, Brady." Mr. Lovejoy tapped his desktop, the sound thudding through the room.

"Yes sir." Brady crossed his arms.

"Because I want you to write the article's first draft. Then I'll review it and add my own touches."

"All right. Just so you know, I may not be able to replicate Mr. Weld's passion."

Mr. Lovejoy's finger stilled. "And why's that?"

"Well, I'm more of a neutral observer. I'm still formulating my thoughts on all this."

At his comment, Charlotte frowned, then turned away.

"Just write it. We're supposed to be objective. If need be, I'll add the passion. I'm good at that." He smirked. "Can you have something by tomorrow afternoon?"

"Sure, you can count on it."

"Well, I've got plenty of other work to do, so I'll be in my office with the door closed."

As their boss left, Charlotte remained staring at Brady.

"What?" he finally asked.

"I can't believe you." Her lips pressed tight.

"You know I want all blacks to have more rights and to be treated well," Brady said. "I just don't know how we get there."

Charlotte rubbed the back of her neck.

"You won't believe how a black man has ruined my life, Char. I ran into this fellow who was a steward on the steamboat I took to Cincinnati. I was interviewing to become a cub pilot for Captain Price, and he messed it all up. My dreams are dashed once again!"

"That's a shame. Does Mr. Lovejoy know you were looking for a new job?"

"No. My heart has always been with the steamboat. He and you both know that, but I didn't tell him. The opportunity just presented itself. After all, I'm just an apprentice here."

A gentleman came through the front door and approached Charlotte's desk.

"Hello," he said. "I'm Owen Lovejoy. Is Parrish available?"

"Parrish?"

"Oh, I'm sorry." He chuckled. "I'm Parrish's brother. That's what we call him within the family. Is Elijah available? I've brought him a roll and just wanted to visit a short time."

"Well, good to meet you, sir. I'm Charlotte, and that's Brady over there. I know he's quite busy, but I imagine he can make time for his brother. I'll check." A few moments later, she waved Owen to Mr. Lovejoy's office, then disappeared into a back room.

She returned with the copy of *Robinson Crusoe* and a broad smile. "You won't believe what I figured out about this book." She waved it in the air over her head.

"What?"

"Mr. Lovejoy signed it."

"No! How can that be?"

"Look for yourself." She opened to the inscription.

"It's signed 'Parrish L.' We now know who Parrish is."

"Really! Can't believe it." He grabbed the book from her hands. "Amazing. So this book was signed by Mr. Lovejoy, but who is this William he gave it to?"

"We'll have to ask him directly." She looked back at his office. "But only after Owen Lovejoy leaves."

Once Mr. Lovejoy was free, they both charged into his office. He sat with a smirk on his face, his tongue contentedly tracing his lips after his last bite of sweet roll. Brady blurted out, "Sorry to bother you, sir, but do you remember this book I saved from the Tecumseh disaster? Looks like it has your signature in it— Parrish L."

"No! Let me see that." Mr. Lovejoy snatched the book and fumbled to find the spot in the first few pages. "You're right. This is the one I gave to William. Unbelievable."

"Who's William?" Charlotte queried.

Brady reached for a chair and sank into it. Charlotte remained standing, her arms crossed. Mr. Lovejoy went on to explain that William was Sandford's given name, but it had been taken away from him by an early owner. While he served as an apprentice with Mr. Lovejoy and Charlotte at the *St. Louis Times,* the book became a useful tool to help him learn to read and write. Mr. Lovejoy had signed it "Parrish," using his second name, to match using a different name for Sandford, namely William. The two had laughed about it at the time—both using an alias.

"Sandford was a real gem. I was so fond of him," Charlotte mused with gleaming eyes. She related to Brady how Sandford had been the most wonderful person to work with. But after a fight with some local boys and a beating by one of their parents, he'd been forced to leave to recuperate.

"I do not know his whereabouts. But I sure wish I did," she lamented as a grim twist overtook her mouth.

In a daze, Brady let his chin lower to his chest. His shoulders drooped as his arms fell over the armrests, lifeless.

"Brady, are you all right?" Mr. Lovejoy half-rose from his chair.

"Incredible," Brady muttered. "I think I've recently run into that guy." He exhaled loudly as he shook his head.

"Where's he at? Tell us!" Charlotte beseeched, her eyes brightening as she leaned over Brady.

"I wish I could." He buried his head in his hands.

* * * * *

Sandford's chest heaved as he came to a staggering stop. The tree trunks surrounding him were of great comfort. Like good friends, they would guard him, keeping the howling hounds away.

Wouldn't they?

His heart fluttered. Of course not. But what now? It would take more than a few minutes to recover from the relentless running. His weary legs finally said enough, and he slumped to the ground. He rubbed his numb hands and blew into them with what little breath he could summon. Icy sweat trickled down his ribcage.

Would it be best to stay in friendly confines or go back to the road? Shafts of the sun's rays were now finding their way into the woods. Sweat beaded like morning dew on his forehead. His eyelids felt heavy. Was it from eyelashes crusted over with frost, or was he just that tired? This was the time he was supposed to be sleeping. No, he couldn't stay here. He must find another barn—one where a friendly owner wouldn't cater to the likes of a bounty hunter with bloodhounds chomping at the bit.

He staggered to his feet and trudged on past the trees through the high brush. If he should die in trying to become a free man, so be it. One hour of virtuous liberty was worth an eternity of bondage.

One thing was for sure. He must resist thoughts of feeling sorry for himself. Visions of his mother and sister slaving in the fields took over. How were their bodies holding up? Were their backs bearing red stripes from a whip when bodies couldn't keep up? Oh, how in his solitude he missed them—now so far away. He said a prayer.

The dog yapping carried by the wind became louder. He wasn't moving fast enough. He pushed the briars and bramble aside with renewed vigor. Back to the road, he must go. Finding his way there was the only answer. But each stride felt more wobbly as his legs were weak and he teetered on numb feet.

The shadows gave way to a brightness. Following the light, he sensed a clearing. Could the roadway be just ahead? Yes, there it was. *Praise God.* Would this be his path to safety?

The rhythm of clomping hooves in the wind told him a rider would soon be upon him. He looked back at the bend in the road. No sign of them yet. Should he dart back into the woods? No. Soon the rider appeared, and the rhythm continued unabated. The rider passed without a word.

After what seemed like two miles down the road, Sandford came upon a man working on his fence. In the distance behind him stood a red barn with a white farmhouse, a row of stately trees protecting its west side.

He had no choice. He must risk talking to the man. "Kind sir, I am a steamboat steward who has fallen into hard times. I am freezing and tired. Could you see it in your heart to let me sleep a few hours in your barn?"

The man did not respond immediately but finished tightening the barbed wire around a post. He then set his tool down and cast a look to the sky before staring into Sandford's eyes.

"I sense you are a good man. You sound like one, anyway. I don't want to know anything about your background. Yes, you can stay in the barn, but if I find you've stolen something, I'll come after you. Understand?"

"Bless you, sir. Mister . . . ?"

"Riggins."

"Believe me, don't worry about the stealing." The last thing I want is another person chasing me.

* * * * *

Sandford had hoped the inside of the barn would be warmer. But getting out of the wind was a most welcome benefit, even though it meant trading fresh air for musty barn air. His eyes darted from one corner to another, trying to identify objects, but they were all shrouded in darkness. A single window high up in the back of the loft was the only source of light. Could he muster the strength to climb up there? Imagining the soft hay that must await him above, he strode toward the ladder.

As he looked down to find the first rung, a narrow shaft of light caught something familiar in a wooden box behind the ladder. He had seen his father use them. An animal trap, taking a winter hiatus, collected dust in the box. Thinking nothing further, he took a few steps up the ladder. Then he heard the very muffled howl of the hounds in the distance. *Wait—it's either me or them, is it not?* He stepped back down and pulled the trap from the box, studying in particular its release mechanism. *But what to use for the bait?*

The faint smell of the sausage he had put in his pocket wafted up into his nostrils. No, he needed it for later. How could he forgo the sustenance of that piece of meat on a hunch some hound dog might be attracted to the trap?

He pulled the sausage out of his pocket and opened the napkin around it. How could something so dried and shriveled look so appetizing? For a few anxious moments he froze with indecision. Then he returned it to his pocket. But five seconds later, he dug it out once again. He took a bite and attached the remaining piece to the trap.

Sandford positioned the trap just inside the front door. With new energy, he mounted the ladder to the loft to find a spot in the hay. How sweet would the smell be, and how soft would the hay feel under his weary head.

Sometime later, a pounding of nails around the front door awakened him from his brief sleep. What was happening? Was Riggins securing the door so he couldn't get out? Had he outsmarted him with his own kind of trap? Who would get there first, the bounty hunter with his dogs, or the local lawman?

Chapter 11

Brady was in no mood to be spending their day off making this little journey. He had to admit, though, it felt good to have Char right behind him, her arms clutching his belly, as they rode atop Patches on their way into the country.

The gentle clomping of the mare's hooves on the hard-packed roadway and the warmth from the sun high above brought some peace, but not enough to settle his troubled mind.

"If Malcolm did anywhere near the job he did on this bridle, I'll be so pleased," Charlotte offered.

"We can only imagine," Brady mumbled.

"I've decided this is the thing I want you to spend your money on. That was so generous of you to offer to buy me a really special gift for my birthday."

"What? Wait. Why didn't you say something earlier? I don't have much money with me."

"That's all right. I'm sure Malcolm's boss won't mind if you pay him later. They've been good family friends for a long time. I can't wait for you to meet Malcolm."

As they entered the shop, Malcolm peered up from his workbench. He set down his tool, stood, and walked over to greet them; his bright smile framed by a handsome black face.

"Malcolm, I'd like you to meet my good friend, Brady."

Malcolm extended his arm to shake, but Brady looked down.

"I've heard a lot about your talent," Brady mumbled as he searched the floor with his eyes.

"Thanks. Let me show you what I've made for Miss Charlotte here." He yelled out, "Samuel, will you bring the saddle over here, please?" Samuel picked up the saddle near a far wall and carried it over.

"This is my older brother, Samuel," Malcolm said. Brady nodded as the young man handed Charlotte the saddle, his smile revealing a chipped tooth.

"Oh my, Malcolm, it's beautiful! What a rich color. See, Brady, this is small enough to fit behind yours, and it's English style without a horn. This was Malcolm's idea." Charlotte's face radiated as she stepped over to pat Malcolm on the back, drawing a modest chuckle from him.

"Very nice, Malcolm," Brady said. "You've obviously pleased Charlotte." Brady turned to Samuel. "Your brother seems to know what he's doing, doesn't he, Samuel?"

"No doubt 'bout it. Wish I could do that!" Samuel beamed.

"How much do we owe you?" Brady asked Malcolm.

"Boss said it should run about fifteen dollars."

Brady's heart rumbled deep. The twenty-five dollars his father had given him from his mother's savings was long gone. He dreaded thinking about in whose pocket that money now resided.

* * * * *

That he would lay awake tossing and turning didn't surprise Brady. Two years was not a long time to forget something as traumatic as the explosion and his mother's death. But why did this fellow Sandford or William—whatever his name was—play such a central role in his life? He'd never forget him. Nor could he forgive him. But by all accounts, he was not an evil fellow. He didn't deserve to die. Brady shuddered thinking how easily he had handed over a significant sum—twenty-five dollars to help fund some bounty hunter's relentless pursuit. Money that was once earmarked for Charlotte.

It was better to think of something less upsetting, like watching the shoreline of the river glide by and reading the river with a head full of experience. There was nothing like hearing the steamboat's whistle or the pilot call out, "Stop the starboard wheel. Bring her around." How rewarding it was to feel the stern come around right where she was expected to. Order on the river was supposed to happen, not chaos. That's what life on the Mississippi was all about. Bringing order to an ever-changing vista. Would he ever be in that pilothouse again?

* * * * *

Riggins finished pounding in the last of the nails securing his barn door. No doubt, he felt sympathetic to the stranger's plight. This was a free state. Slave or not, the man didn't deserve to be chased down like an animal. He gathered up his toolbox, remaining nails, and boards, and took one final look as far as he could see. The light wind carried a faint howling. Off to the west, where the view of the long road going by his place ended with a bend, there was no sign yet of the dogs.

Meanwhile, he'd sit in a rocking chair on his porch and do something worthwhile—a good opportunity to sharpen his tools. But before starting, he'd secure his shotgun and have it at the ready. Who knew what was about to happen?

About a half hour later, a haggard-looking man with a floppy hat and four-day beard approached his porch, a piece of towel dangling from his belt. The man's dog pulled at its leash, his howling making talking difficult. The air grew menacing.

"What's your business?" Riggins yelled out.

"Quiet now, Buddy. Time to quit your yapping." The man tried to hush his dog with a sharp yank on the leash, a rifle in his other hand. "I'm chasin' down a fugitive slave. Gonna bring him back to his master." He spit off to the side, a toothpick somehow still twitching at the other side of his mouth.

"Well, I'll be." Riggins dropped his file and tool into their box and lifted his shotgun to his lap. "So, where's your other hounds? Heard more than this one all morning." He rocked back slightly in his chair.

"Sad story. Had to leave him by the side of the road a ways back." The man shook his head. "Couldn't keep up. His time was done." He tilted his head back. "Fetch, find, found. I'm a lovin' my hounds," he sang out. His dog strained toward the barn. "So, you seen a slave hereabouts? Buddy's saying he's real close."

"Can't say as I have, but then we are a free state, so I don't pay attention. I've had some theft of late. Had no choice but to nail shut the barn door." The creaking boards under his rocking chair revealed another spot in need of nails, but not today.

"Is that so? You wouldn't mind if I looked around, would ya?"

"Well, it is my private property, ya know. Maybe I don't want you a meddlin' in my stuff." His hand clutched his shotgun tighter.

The man's eyebrows lifted as a sneer formed across his grizzled face. He raised his hat and scratched his head. "Ya don't say. Well, I'm not a bettin' man." He spit, and the toothpick twitched. "But I am willing to bet you won't risk your life over me just takin' a gander in that barn over yonder."

The rocking chair stopped. After an extended silence, Riggins concluded the man was right. No sense taking risks.

"Well, I s'pose it don't hurt for you to take a look. But I ain't helpin' you. If yer that determined, you'll have to break in yerself." He resumed rocking. "I'm staying out of it."

The man stormed toward the barn, echoing his apparent favorite refrain with a sing-song rhythm: "Fetch, find, found. I'm a lovin' my hounds." After a moment, he yelled back, "Ya got a crowbar?"

"Inside the barn," Riggins answered while turning away with a smirk.

During the next half hour, Riggins figured he'd never heard as many curse words fly out of a man's mouth.

* * * * *

"It's so much more comfortable to have a saddle back here, Brady." Charlotte gave Brady a gentle squeeze on his shoulders from behind. They were on their way to her house after a full day at the newspaper.

"Good thing Mr. Sinclair said I can pay him a few dollars each month."

"Mama's going to be so happy to have you fix that wobbly table leg. In fact, she insists you stay for dinner."

"I suppose," he mumbled. "I did tell my father I'd be late." He gave Patches a kick, and the horse responded with a faster gait.

Soon they arrived at the small brown house. The wooden stoop creaked as they stepped up through the front door. *Another thing to add to Brady's list,* Charlotte thought.

Mama hurried over to give Brady a big hug. He looked like a small wiener lost in an oversized bun, hoping to get squeezed out.

"What's the matter, Brady? Don't you like a little lovin' from my mama?"

Brady responded only with a hard swallow, averted eyes, and a half-smile.

"So good to see you again, Brady," Rosetta proclaimed with a big grin as she took a stride back. "Charlotte has nothing but good things to say about you. Hope you can fix this table." She gestured with a heavy hand laid atop the table, and it wobbled mightily.

"I'll do my best. I brought my hand drill and some extra screws, but I'm no cabinet maker." An almost too-quick smile flashed, then disappeared.

"No worries," Rosetta said. "Just so it's sturdy and you're done by dinner time. Wouldn't want all my fine fixin's to end up on the floor, would we?" A heavy laugh escaped from deep within her.

"Oh, Mama. Don't put any pressure on him. So, anyway, what sort of fine fixin's are you fixin' to make?"

"Chitlins with collard greens. Then I already baked a sweet potato pie settin' on the counter over there."

"Mmm. Oh, Mama. I can't wait. God only knows how much I love that."

"Anything for my sweet child and her good friend." She removed a lid from a pan and stirred.

"Well, Mrs. Jones, pie sounds wonderful. The sooner I get your table fixed, the sooner we'll all get a piece. Char, will you please help me turn it over on the floor?" His lips pressed together.

Once Brady got started with the table, Charlotte joined her mother to help prepare dinner.

"Mama, you wouldn't believe the article Brady wrote for Mr. Lovejoy," she whispered into her mother's ear. "About some of the ridiculous laws our people been suffering with over all these years."

"Is that right?" her mama said loud enough for Brady's ears to perk up, as he was rather close by.

"I was braggin' about you, Brady." Charlotte turned to him with a big smile.

* * * * *

No sooner had they sat down to eat, Mrs. Jones asked Brady about the laws impacting her people.

Brady looked down at his plate, glad he could talk a moment and not dig right in. He couldn't decide which looked less appealing. For sure, neither aroma was winning him over.

"If we lived in Virginia, for example, Charlotte here, even as a free colored person, would be subject to twenty lashes if she went to a school to learn to read or write," Brady said. "She and I have been working together on that." He ventured a small bite of the collard greens and chewed cautiously.

"Here in Missouri," Charlotte piped in, "somebody like Malcolm, if he disobeyed his boss, could be thrown in jail for as long as his boss felt necessary."

Mrs. Jones just shook her head back and forth. It kept shaking as she lowered her eyes to Brady's plate.

"Land sakes, boy. You must not like my cookin'."

With a slight squirm, Brady looked down at the chitlins he had pushed off to one side. "Sorry, Mrs. Jones. I'm not all that hungry today." After a few moments of probing eyes from both Mrs. Jones and Charlotte, he admitted he wasn't used to this kind of food.

"Mama." Charlotte tapped her mother's hand, drawing her frowning attention. "On a more cheerful note, I have some exciting news about Mr. Lovejoy. He's getting married!" she squealed.

"Oh, when?" Brady sat up straighter.

"April. Can't come soon enough!"

"What's her name?" asked Mrs. Jones, her eyes sparkling.

Charlotte's face radiated. "Celia Ann."

"Oh, that's a pretty name," came her throaty note of approval.

"First, he finishes seminary. Now he plans to get married. Sounds like he's got his life pointed in a positive direction," Brady added.

"Yeah, if only the newspaper was doing better," Charlotte mumbled. "With little advertising, he says we're losing money each month. He doesn't know if he'll be able to keep us on."

"I liked it better when you were talking about the wedding, Char." Brady leaned back in his chair, the thought of food having escaped his mind, to his great joy.

Chapter 12

Not until midday on his sixth day of travels did Sandford realize a long time had passed since he heard the howling. Leaving his sausage on the trap he had spotted in Riggins's barn must have done the trick. If only his jump from the upper window had not resulted in a sore ankle that slowed him down. And now a heavy cold rain drenched him. He became a walking icicle and could go no farther. Fortunately, he found another barn in which to take shelter. But for that and the providence of God, he figured he'd have frozen to death. He prayed that God would also provide some friendly soul to rescue him. By nighttime, he had dried out enough and gathered the strength to forge on.

But his stride now seemed shorter. His legs numb, he could not discern a difference from the feel of his movements. Nor, looking down, could he detect it visually in the dim starlight. But he knew it. Each step, indeed, was getting shorter—more precious and dear.

Along the road, a horse-drawn buggy approached. He ducked back into the woods. Soon thereafter, a man on horseback appeared. *I must be getting closer to where more people live.* Sandford started to call out, only to have his voice fade, overtaken by doubt and fear. But now, when an elderly man leading a white horse approached, he had another sense—this time warming his heart. The man wore a distinguished hat and long overcoat. *He must be the person I've been hoping for.*

"Are you a slave?" His voice was like an angel's, floating in on ice crystals, melting with grace.

"Well, er, I am sick. Do you know anyone who could help me?" Sandford's face tightened.

"But are you a slave?" Truth—that's no doubt what the man's eyes searched for from beneath his broad-brimmed hat.

"Yes sir. I am." *There, I have said it.* A pain lingered in the back of his throat. "Can you please help me?"

"What is your name?"

What name shall I use? "William is the name given me by my mama, but since a child, everyone's called me Sandford."

"All right, William. Let me tell you what I'm going to do. I want to go home and get my covered carriage. Wait right here. I'll be back."

After the man departed, William paced at the edge of the woods. Could this man be trusted? Would he return with the authorities to arrest him and whisk him away? Dashing his hopes for freedom? *I would rather die than go back to slavery!*

After over an hour of fretting, William watched the buggy slowly pull up. He tentatively stepped inside, settled into his seat, closed his eyes, and tipped his head back. They were underway, together. What had been a constant tremble to his hands now eased.

"What's your last name?" the man asked.

"I don't have one I use, sir." He thought about how he'd rather be called Friday than take the name of one of his masters.

Upon arrival at the man's house, William hesitated to go in, but couldn't say no to the entreaties of the man's wife. As he sat by the fire while the lady prepared some food, his feet burned with revitalized circulation. He could not help but think of the passage from Matthew in the Bible that said: "For I was hungry and you gave me something to eat, I was thirsty and you gave me something to drink, I was a stranger and you invited me in." Jesus had finished by saying, "Truly I tell you, whatever you did for one of the least of these brothers and sisters of mine, you did for me" (Matt. 25:35–40).

William was summoned to the table and sat dumbfounded when he realized a white woman was actually serving a black man. He worried that he might not be polite enough, then found his head slowly shaking in disbelief. At first he could not eat, but after a while, he was able to reacquaint his stomach with the benefits of nutrition.

The old man raised the question of his last name. "William," he said, clearing his throat. "My name is Wells Brown. What shall we call you?" He leaned in, bright-eyed.

"Well, sir, since you are the first person in a long time to befriend me, I'll give you the privilege of picking a name. I do, however, insist on retaining my birth name, William."

"I'm happy to name you after me then." The man's face beamed.

"I like the sound of William Wells Brown." William took a deep satisfied breath. "So be it."

He ended up staying with the Browns about a fortnight. They made him some clothes and bought him a new pair of boots. Upon leaving, he reflected on how kind they had been, how they had treated him as if he were their own child. He hoped he would run into others as nice on his way to Canada.

I am a free man now! His pulse raced, and he felt a lightness in his chest like never before. If only his mother, sister, and friends could experience such a feeling as well.

Chapter 13

Summer 1834

Late on a quiet July afternoon, bold shafts of light shone through the newspaper office window. Brady sat at his desk reviewing a copy for the next day's newspaper. Charlotte was in the back working at her sewing table.

A middle-aged lady with a bonnet and voluminous skirt sashayed through the front door. Marching right up to Brady, she demanded, "Where's Charlotte?" as she collapsed her sun parasol brusquely.

"She's still in the back, ma'am. Should be done pretty soon. May I ask what this is about?"

"Word around town is she has some new gadget she sews with. I must see it."

"Well, why don't I go ask her if she has some time to visit with you?" He offered a pleasant smile.

"Ask her? No, I'll go right to her, myself." Her eyebrows drew closer.

"But ma'am, if you don't know where you're going, you might soil that pretty dress of yours. Printing is done back there with a lot of black ink. Heaven forbid if you got some on you."

"I can take care of my dress just fine, thank you." She reached down to adjust it at the waist. "Just tell me where to go." She forced a parting smile.

"Go through that door, veer right, and head to the far corner." He pinched his lips together to stop a heavy sigh. "She has a table there."

* * * * *

Charlotte raised her head up from reviewing her customer list. The woman approaching looked like she belonged at a parade, not the back of a workshop.

"Charlotte Jones?" The woman deposited her parasol on the desk.

Charlotte cautiously answered, "Yes ma'am. And you are?"

"Francis Dithers. I hear tell you have some sort of machine that sews. Is that true?"

"Yes ma'am. It's over there on the side table. Mr. Lovejoy got it for me. I just put it away for the day."

Mrs. Dithers' brow furrowed.

"Otherwise, I'd show you how it works. I was just going over my customer list here."

"Let me see that." Mrs. Dithers snatched the list from her hand. "I'm a seamstress too, if that's what you call yourself. You better not have any of my customers on your list." She held the list close to a lantern on the table and perused down.

"Well, I'll be!" She gave a gasp. "Mrs. Bixby is here . . . and there's Mrs. Riley. Oh no! Denise Witherspoon—she's a good friend of mine." She slammed the list back on the table. "I should say she was a good friend of mine." She stomped her foot and looked away.

"I'm sorry to upset you, Mrs. Dithers, but I ask you to think about it a minute. There are times when a machine like this can save a person both time and money." Charlotte nodded affirmatively trying to sway Mrs. Dithers' feelings.

"How's that? Nothing can compare with the artistry and quality of my hand stitching. I take great pride in it." The woman held her chin high, followed by a heavy sigh.

"That may be true, but on many occasions, time is what matters. I can charge my customers less this way." Charlotte tried to offer a conciliatory smile.

"Fiddlesticks! I'll take hand craftsmanship over a machine any day. You must stop stealing my customers! Do you hear me?"

"Yes, I'm sorry, Mrs. Dithers. Sometimes we just have to change along with how the world is changing. We may not all like it, but it usually benefits most of us in the end." Charlotte figured that pretty much said it all. This was all minor compared to other changes that needed acceptance.

"Well, I, for one, do not like it." Mrs. Dithers grabbed her parasol, turned with a huff, and stormed out. "Not one bit!" was her parting remark.

* * * * *

As Brady sat in the newspaper office awaiting the arrival of Mr. Lovejoy from an out-of-town trip, he fretted over his latest copy of the story. The happenings of the previous day had been so monumental that his retelling, even though based on first-hand accounts, couldn't do the event justice.

Mr. Lovejoy stormed through the door. "I never knew human beings could still be so barbaric," he said, his eyes wet and swollen. He clutched at his collar to loosen it. "Burning another human being at the stake? This isn't the dark ages!"

"I know," Brady said. "I got sick just listening to people retell what happened. I've tried to recapture it in this draft of an article." He banged his knuckles on the copy laying on his desk.

"I just passed by the site, and people told me that afterward, boys were throwing stones at the remaining skull, trying to see who could break it first."

Brady shuddered, thinking back to the days when he was such a stone thrower, not too unlike these boys. Shame. *Nothing but haunting shame ravaged me from within.* There was no other way to think about it. He slumped deep down into his chair.

"Let me see what you've written." Mr. Lovejoy gazed around the room, then reached for the copy. "Where's Charlotte?"

"When I stopped by to pick her up, she said she was so upset she couldn't come to work today."

After several minutes of reading while still standing, Mr. Lovejoy tossed the copy back onto Brady's desk. "This needs more passion. I'll have to work on it. I've got plenty of that now." He stomped to the window and gazed out. "Do we know anything more about the circumstances? How did McIntosh's killing the police officer come about?"

"Not sure, sir. But no doubt, that's what riled up the crowd, especially with the policeman's widow being a cripple and all. It's unfortunate all around." He paused, pulling in a deep breath as he shook his head. "They say there were thousands, and some just decided to take justice into their own hands."

"And McIntosh ends up getting burned at the stake." Mr. Lovejoy looked upward. "God rest his soul. God help us all!"

* * * * *

For the next several weeks, Mr. Lovejoy penned blistering editorials in the Observer. He described the recent events as "savage barbarity" and encouraged all those who had been involved to come forward and seek forgiveness.

The judge in the case, Luke Lawless, shocked many—not only in the region, but also across the country—when he gave his instructions to the grand jury. He told them that although McIntosh's death was a tragedy and violated the law, because it was perpetrated by thousands, it was beyond the reach of human law.

Lawless went on to blame Mr. Lovejoy's editorials for stirring up a frenzy amongst the community. When the Observer argued that slavery was a sin that should be abolished, Lawless maintained Mr. Lovejoy's position was only stirring the slaves to revolt. The judge acknowledged the right of freedom of the press, but questioned why society should be a victim of "sanctimonious madmen." The grand jury found no one guilty.

A young state legislator from Illinois, Abraham Lincoln, condemned the substitution of "wild and furious passions" for the law.

Mr. Lovejoy was so moved by all that had happened that he sank into a severe depressive state, feeling personally responsible. He went as far as to say he did not deserve to live. He would rather "be chained to the same tree as McIntosh and share his fate." He felt the judge's ruling encouraged mob violence and went on to editorialize that he'd rather have the office of the Observer "scattered in fragments to the four winds" than accept the doctrines promoted by Judge Lawless.

* * * * *

As expected, mob action became the order of the day. One night, a group of people ransacked the printing office. The following morning, Charlotte began to clean up with Brady as Mr. Lovejoy surveyed the shambles of the room. She kneeled to pick up scattered type strewn across the floor. Then the thought of her sewing machine flashed into her head. She jumped to her feet. *Had they ransacked that?* She dashed toward the back room. A quick glance toward the far corner caught a pile of fabrics stacked high on her table. She pushed them aside to find her sewing machine still intact. *What a relief!* Charlotte gently patted it, pulled in a breath, then collapsed into her chair, a loud exhale escaping through twitching lips. She took a few moments to settle her grateful heart, then returned to the front room.

Mr. Lovejoy sat at Brady's desk, his head in his hands.

"They're only material things," Brady consoled him from behind, his hand on his shoulder. "That trunk of clothing, the furniture—what a shame, though, I know that was new."

"Wait a minute," Mr. Lovejoy exclaimed while standing abruptly. "That box of wedding gifts. It was right beside my desk." He rushed back to his office, Charlotte and Brady close at his heels.

"Gone! Those wretched scoundrels!" He slumped in his desk chair and cast his gaze to the heavens.

"This makes a decision for me much easier," he proclaimed, pounding his fist on the desk. He peered into the eyes of first Brady, and then Charlotte. "I've been thinking about making the move to the free state of Illinois." He exhaled deeply. "Should be a bit calmer over there. Brady, I know this isn't your long-term dream job, but I could really use your help if you could somehow stick it out until we get over the hump. I will not let them stop me." He stood up and straightened his back. "I have every right to print my views in this country. I want to start again in Alton, Illinois. It's only a short ways up the river, but on the free side. Seems to make a lot of sense. Are you with me?"

"Amen, sir." Brady's eyes widened. "I do have an uncle who lives up that way. I'm sure he'd let me stay with him—at least for a while."

"What about you, Charlotte? You've been awfully quiet."

"I don't know, sir. I do have some cousins around there. Maybe. Would I be able to run my sewing business up there? Come to think of it, the likes of Mrs. Dithers wouldn't be around to pester me."

"Of course. I wouldn't have gone to all the trouble to secure you that new invention for nothing."

Her eyebrows lowered as her brow furrowed. "To be honest with you, my head's just not thinking. Ever since the McIntosh tragedy, I've been in a state of shock." Inwardly, she reflected on how guilty she felt for thinking about her sewing business before Mr. Lovejoy's overwhelming issues.

* * * * *

Several Sundays later, the late-July sun was making for a steamy day as Brady walked sprightly from church with Uncle Raymond and Aunt Shirley. Passersby tipped their hats, saying, "Good day."

"Alton sure seems to be a bustling town," Brady said. "How many people do you suppose live here?"

"I figure there's now more than twenty-five hundred people and fifty stores." Uncle Raymond grasped his wife's elbow to help her over a protruding tree root blocking the pathway. "I think there's a good future here. I know my wood supply business with the steamboats is sure thriving."

"Maybe that's what I should be doing just to be close up to those beauties." A vision of being on a wood supply scow in his failed pursuit of Sandford flashed across, then right out of, his mind. "At least, I get to go down to the wharf tomorrow to unload Mr. Lovejoy's new press off the Palmyra. It actually is due in to-day, but Mr. Lovejoy doesn't want us dealing with it on a Sunday. Tomorrow's the big day."

After a few moments of walking in silence, Aunt Shirley tipped her bonnet-shaded face his way, little blond curls fringing her forehead. "So, Brady, how are you liking our church after a few weeks?"

"Fine. I've met some nice people more my age." Brady smiled as he spotted a family with a couple more teens ahead of them. He wished his aunt and uncle would speed up their gait so they'd catch up.

"Today's sermon surprised me, though."

"How's that?" Aunt Shirley's brow furrowed, crinkling up under those silly curls. Behind them, the church tower's bell tolled noon.

"Well, I'm surprised a pastor in a free state would use the Bible to defend slavery."

His uncle looked away and then back while scratching his head. "There's no doubt there were plenty of instances of it way back in those days of the Mosaic law. From the early days, slavery was not denounced." He hastened his steps.

Brady turned quiet, his mind not wanting to process further. Just when he thought he was getting to know his relatives, they now seemed foreign. Now his steps indeed were less sprightly, the sun less bright.

* * * * *

On Monday morning, just after the clock struck 7:00 a.m., Brady hurried down to the wharf with some other strong lads to retrieve the new press from the Palmyra.

It soon became evident that some dastardly mischief had been perpetrated the night before. Some people were gawking and pointing out along the shore of the Mississippi.

"No, no!" Brady yelled out. "This can't be. We're in the free state of Illinois now!" Fear trickled up his throat. He caught his breath, then stomped anxiously to the shoreline, the tips of his boots now wet. He could hardly believe what his eyes now focused on. Not furniture, or even wedding gifts. A gray crown-like piece of metal stood up just above the water's rippling surface, an iceberg of steel surely anchoring it from below. Must have taken several men to muscle that hunk of a press. It now lay still at a most unwelcome resting place—the bottom of the river.

Brady stared down and shook his head in search of some answer. A hand-sized stone lay at his feet. He picked it up and flung it as far as he could out into the river, hoping the magnitude of its splash would somehow be as great as his outrage. "You're what belongs in the water!" he shouted.

The press was not salvageable. This time, Mr. Lovejoy's fortitude could not overcome the stark reality. He would break down weeping, inconsolable. His hopes and dreams were drowning in intolerance.

Chapter 14

Several days later Brady sat with Charlotte in the office listening intently as Mr. Lovejoy tried to bring focus to their efforts in light of the recent setbacks. His arms waved, conveying an extra bit of unleashed emotion.

"We will continue to be primarily a religious newspaper promoting missionary work and personal repentance." The man's round face somehow appeared gaunt on this day, his full lips pressed flat. Even the fluffy wave of hair at the front top of his head lacked its normal buoyancy. "I have some additional financial backing in that regard. But that does not mean I'll remain silent when it comes to slavery. It is an awful evil and sin. In addition, under no circumstances will I give up the right of conscience, the freedom of opinion, and freedom of the press."

"But sir?" Char scooted to the edge of her chair. "Are we not missing a key ingredient—a press?" Her big black shoes planted firmly on the floor, she tapped a pencil against a notepad.

"For the time being, the good people at the *Alton Telegraph* have agreed to print the *Observer* for us. Bless them. A new press is due in September."

"I do wonder about your family." Charlotte smoothed her cotton skirt over her knees—a simple affordable skirt not nearly as nice as some she sewed. She folded her hands on her lap. "How's Celia Ann holding up under all this?"

"Amazingly well, considering her health problems. She's never whispered a hint of discontent at all the hardships we've had to endure." He reached to twist his wedding ring around his finger. "Despite people shunning and hating me, she has devotedly stuck by my side, clinging to me more closely than ever. What a strong woman. What a blessing God has provided to me!"

"Very impressive. It's just too bad so many people around here are not receptive to your antislavery message," Brady said. He tried to picture a map of Illinois in his mind. "Maybe we need to move farther north?"

"I'm in no mood to move again." Mr. Lovejoy jutted out his jaw and pursed his lips, the resolve in his sparkling eyes now appearing as hard as diamonds. "We've got to make it work here." His chest heaved, then contracted. Like a dog protecting its territory, his muscles seemed coiled at the ready for the fight.

Brady rubbed his throbbing temples, drawing a deep breath. "It doesn't help when pastors, like the one at my uncle's church, say slavery was in the Bible, so it must be OK."

"He and others like him are misguided, son." Mr. Lovejoy pressed his lips together and looked each of them squarely in the eye. "There's a difference between providing servitude for a period of time for a fee, like in biblical days, and the slavery of today. Modern slavery is chattel slavery where people are deemed possessions that can be bought and sold. As a possession, they can be treated any way the owner sees fit."

"But a lot of owners treat their slaves quite well," Brady responded. "I can see how they became content with that." He closed a folder on his desk and set it aside.

"True, but they're still denying black people their basic right of freedom." Mr. Lovejoy headed toward his office but then spun back around with authority. "Jesus proclaimed for all of us a common brotherhood as children of God. The apostle Paul said in Galatians, '[T]here is neither Jew nor Greek, there is neither slave nor free, there is no male and female, for you are all one in Christ Jesus.'"

* * * * *

As Brady left the office later with Charlotte, her silence surprised him. A curious detachment wandered in her eyes. He nudged her arm with his elbow. "Why so quiet, Char?"

"Never mind me. You just go on by yourself." She tilted her chin down and frowned.

"Why?" He shuffled back a step. "What's the matter?"

"I think I've finally figured you out, Brady Scott. Why don't you just call me Friday? And I can start calling you Robinson Crusoe."

"What?" He tripped over one foot, rocked to a halt, and whirled toward her.

"You treat me so nice all the time. It's not because you're fond of me."

Huh? He blinked at her. Her hands clasped her waist each side, her elbows jutting out. "What are you talking about? I adore you!" He reached for her hand, but she guarded hers.

"I heard it in your voice with Mr. Lovejoy. Everything is OK if you treat us black folks nice. Or if we're white enough and not too black. Don't you think I remember that time you didn't shake Malcolm's hand? Then when Mama tried to give you a big hug, you couldn't get out of her grasp fast enough!"

"Char, please . . . I just wasn't comfortable." He released a heavy sigh as his jaw tightened.

"Yeah, because they were too black. You can't get past thinking a black man killed your mother. All this business with Mr. Lovejoy. All you care about is being able to say what you want— freedom of the press. That's all that matters to you! Yeah, it would be nice to get rid of slavery while you're at it. But if not, as long as you're nice to us, it's OK." She wiped tears from her eyes.

Before Brady could craft a response, she had run ahead toward her cousin's home as a steady brisk wind buffeted his sullen face.

* * * * *

Slamming the front door behind him, Brady stormed into his uncle's house and plopped onto the living room sofa.

"I've had it at that newspaper." He scowled at Aunt Shirley, who had come scurrying in from the kitchen. "The *Observer* can get by just fine without me." He punched at a pillow beside him, then punched it again.

"But I thought you so admired Mr. Lovejoy, not to mention that Charlotte girl. You talk about them all the time."

"Well, talk is one thing. They're really looking for a better person at the core."

"Oh, I see," came his aunt's reply even as her forehead knit as if she didn't see at all. "There's some other things going on." She looked off into the distance. "Maybe I'd better round you up something to drink." She headed back to the kitchen.

Brady stared toward the floor. The intricate weaving of the rug his aunt had braided stood out. *Now there was a product of her hard work—something she loved doing.* She returned to the room and handed him a glass.

"Thank you, Auntie." He took a big swallow of lemonade and contemplated. "You know, how did I end up getting stuck in this newspaper business, anyway?"

"Well, we never really know where God is going to put us, do we?" She cocked her head to the side and tried to lock eyes with him.

"Besides, it's become really dangerous." Another large gulp brought a slight gagging reaction to the overly sour lemonade. "You never know what the next mob is going to do! Whatever happened to becoming a steamboat pilot? That was my dream job."

"That's right." She walked to the window and gazed out. After a moment, she turned toward Brady. "Maybe I shouldn't be telling you this now. You'll have to talk to your uncle when he gets home."

"Tell me, Aunt Shirley. Please." He crossed his arms.

"Well, you seemed so intent on following Mr. Lovejoy, we didn't want to confuse matters. After all, you moved all the way up here to live with us."

Brady stomped his foot. "Aunt Shirley!"

"All right. Your uncle's wood business has been going so well, he's invested in another scow. He wants you to be in charge of it."

* * * * *

An arduous trip poling their scow up the Ohio River to Shawneetown had left them all exhausted. Brady slumped down on a burlap bag of cornmeal to rest with two helpers, Jim and Carl, who had just loaded up new provisions into his uncle's scow. They were docked not far from the general store on shore. The smell of burning tobacco from the store clerk's pipe still lingered on his shirt.

"I think that's about all the room we've got for cornmeal. With all the wood and this case of salt beef, I'm sure glad we're headed back downstream."

"When are we supposed to hook up with the Cumberland?" Jim raked his fingers through his thin black hair, leaving wayward strands dangling in the breeze.

"About two hours downstream, so we've got plenty of time." Brady tipped his head up to admire the flight of a golden hawk passing overhead. Being back on the water was a real joy. Developing new business on the Ohio was one of his uncle's goals, and Brady was happy to be a part of that.

"Untie that rope, Carl." Brady hopped to his feet. "Let's cast off. We've got a beautiful day going. Let's take advantage of it." Some wood ducks skimming water's surface took off flying.

Several miles downriver, a strong wind picked up. As they rounded a bend, that wind carried a woman's plaintive voice. Far ahead on the shore, Brady saw her waving to get their attention, her arms crossing back and forth above her attractive head.

"Please help," she cried. "We're desperate. Do you have any food you could spare?" A piece of the woman's torn sleeve flapped in the breeze.

Feeling it worthy to pursue this woman's predicament, Brady motioned for the other fellows to steer ashore.

"Wait here," he instructed. "I'll go check it all out." He jumped on the nearest rock on shore and strode toward the woman.

"Thank you for stopping, kind sir." She tucked in strands of blond hair on each side, but a half-smile revealed crooked and stained teeth.

"What's the problem, ma'am?"

"My family's not doing well. They're all up in the cave. Do you mind stopping in?" She pointed back.

"Cave?" Brady scanned farther up from the shore.

"Yes, this is Cave-in-Rock. They're all up in there. Come with me." Her eyes pleaded.

Watching his steps through the rocky terrain, Brady followed, occasionally looking up to admire the huge cliff set back along the shoreline. Carved into the cliff was indeed an imposing cave. He approached an opening about fifty feet both height and width. Ledges on each side, however, restricted entry. When he stepped inside after the woman, his eyes had a hard time adjusting to the darkness.

The front of the cave was spacious and open. Brady imagined some bats flitting about in the far reaches overhead. The lady led him farther in where some others were talking. Their voices hushed as Brady approached.

A burly man strode forward and greeted him. "Hello, welcome." He stroked his bearded chin, then extended his hand to shake, and Brady obliged. "This is our family," he added with a sweeping gesture of his arm. "Call me Jack."

The flickering light of a couple lanterns revealed several men's intense eyes glaring back at him. Another took a swig from his liquor bottle. There must have been eight of them, with no other women or children. A distinct stench seemingly trapped in the cave forever filled his nostrils.

"So, who are you?" The words seemed to harden beneath Jack's steely stare.

"Brady." He offered a slight smile. "Brady Scott."

"What's you got with you?" Jack spit down in front of Brady's boots.

"What do you mean? On my scow out there?" He motioned toward the river. A couple of fellows stepped to the cave entrance, guarding against any fast exit.

"Yeah, I need you to list everything." Jack's jaw protruded as his eyes latched onto Brady's.

"Well, I've got mostly wood, but also eight sacks of cornmeal." Brady's shoulders tightened.

"That's all?" The width of Jack's grin seemed to match his level of disbelief.

"Oh, also a case of dried beef."

"Hmmm. Sounds pretty tasty." He licked his lips.

"Listen, I can't share much of it. It's committed to a steamboat—the Cumberland."

"Well, ain't that nice. I hate to disappoint all them steamer folks, but what if I was to tell you I need it? I need it all."

"What do you mean?" Brady brought a shaky hand to his forehead. "You're not telling me you'd just take it, are you?"

"I said I need it all. Oh, but not the wood. Got plenty a that." Jack rested his hand on the hilt of a long knife sheathed on his belt. His fingers continued to massage the nub.

"Are you saying you're g-going to st-steal it?" Brady's voice stammered.

"Oh no. I'll pay you for it. I ain't no thief. Let's see, eight bags of cornmeal and a case a beef. I'd say that's worth about fifteen dollars." He lifted his chin high.

Fifteen? At least that was better than stealing. Brady ran a hand through his hair. "But I paid over twenty."

"Ain't that a shame? Fifteen dollars it is." He drew from his pocket a ten-dollar bill and some coins.

Brady turned to the woman who ensnared him in this trap. No sign of compassion softened her face. A smirk took hold as she looked away.

* * * * *

Hours later, Brady caught up with the Cumberland. Jim and Carl worked to tie the scow firmly to the side of the steamboat while it was still in motion. A strong breeze made the task more difficult as it kicked up some choppy waters.

"Glad to see you again, Frank," Brady shouted out.

"Where you been, Brady?" Frank the deck leadman yelled back. "We were gettin' mighty low on wood."

"Sorry, I got held up. I've got plenty of wood for you here." Brady slid his pole out of the way below the far gunwale, as Jim and Carl started unloading. "No food, though."

"What? No food? Captain already told me he's been a tastin' that beef."

"Well, I guess he'll be disappointed, won't he? I couldn't help it. Had to sell it along with the cornmeal to a gang along the way." Brady stepped up on to the steamboat.

"That's a shame." Frank shook his head. "So how much do we owe you for all the wood?"

"Thirty-five."

"I got only a fifty and some smaller bills. Was expectin' to pay for a lot of food too."

"I've got some change." Brady yanked the fifteen dollars he'd received from Jack out of his pocket and handed it over.

Frank was about to pocket it but then stopped—something must have caught his eye. He took a moment to examine the ten-dollar bill and coins, then moved closer to a nearby lantern.

"Woo-eee, Brady. You must have stopped at Cave-in-Rock. I hate to tell you this, but I'm 'fraid you been snookered." He winced, his nose wrinkling.

"What? What are you talking about? You must be pulling my leg . . . " Brady twisted away with a cringe.

"Nope. Sorry, but this money is counterfeit. I can't accept it."

"Let me see it." He snatched the money out of Frank's hands.

"Most people 'round these parts knows all 'bout them river pirates back there in the cave. People stay wide and clear of it."

"Wouldn't you know I'm the one person who didn't know that." He sighed. "'Course, I'm new to these parts." Brady shook his head. "I'll have to make change with my private stash." He pulled some bills from behind his sock. He then returned to the scow and slumped back into his seat.

"Sorry to be bringin' you the bad news." Frank paused to count his money again, then resumed. "Well, maybe I can make up for it."

"How's that?"

"Pilot Tillman wants to talk to you about an opening as a cub pilot." His lips parted to make room for a slow smile.

"I'll say you've made up for it!" Brady jumped back up on board the steamboat and spun around to his helpers. "Wait for me here, boys."

The waters calmed for the first time that day. The sun, now low in the sky, cast an orange glow out upon the newly serene surface.

Chapter 15

A week later, as the Cumberland came upon the first major point north of Memphis, prospective cub pilot Brady asked Pilot Tillman how he wanted to approach it. The late afternoon sun glistened off gently rippling waters ahead. No other boats were in the vicinity. "That's up to you, son. That's why we're going through this little exercise." He scratched the grizzly gray whiskers covering his chin. "I want to see what you know and how much of a gambler you are." A slight giggle escaped through the gap of a missing tooth.

Brady had been along this part of the great Mississippi a few times before, and there was a reef projecting out from the point. Late summer meant lower water levels. Should he go extra wide to show he was careful, or tight to show how much he really knew about the river? He wanted to demonstrate what he really knew. With a steady grip, he turned the wheel starboard and several moments later announced, "I figure we're at about eight feet here, sir."

Pilot Tillman gave him a condescending look. "We'll see." He tugged on the sounding bell rope and poked his head out the pilothouse window looking for a black-faced deckhand.

"Hey, darkie," he yelled out. "Go get me a depth reading off the stick. And make it snappy!"

Soon a shout out of "eight and one half" came back from the deckhand.

Pilot Tillman rotated to Brady. "Pretty good, son. Off by half a foot." He grinned. "Shoot, I'll give you that. I'm impressed. You just might work out, after all." He yawned and returned to his stool as Brady continued to steer.

After about ten minutes, Brady glanced over to see Pilot Tillman's eyes half closed. He'd better make conversation. "So how long did you say until your retirement, sir?"

Pilot Tillman's head jerked up. "What's that?" He rubbed his eyes.

"Your retirement, sir. How long do you have to go?"

"Ten months from last Tuesday. I'm a countin' the days." He smiled, then slid out his watch. "Dod, dern it!" he blurted out. "Late again."

Heaven forbid. Brady double-checked his river surroundings. Had he been going too slow? No, Steven's Point was just ahead on the starboard side.

"Just can't count on those monkeys," Pilot Tillman said while stomping his foot.

"What's the matter, sir?" Brady moved uneasily on his feet, his head darting back to the pilot.

"My coffee. That blamed steward of ours s'posed to bring me my coffee at four thirty sharp. He's six minutes late!"

Just then, the steward popped his head through the pilothouse door, carrying a tray.

"Blazes, boy. Where you been? I knew you couldn't be out pickin' cotton!" Tillman sniggered.

"I'm sorry, sir." The steward handed over a cup to Pilot Tillman and offered one to Brady, who declined.

"Phew." Pilot Tillman spit out his first gulp. "Cold, cold as an Eskimo's big toe."

"Sorry, sir. Thought Miss Sally had turned on the burner." His chin dipped down.

"Horsefeathers! 'Tween the two of yous, can't you figure out if the burner's been turned on?"

"I'll hustle it right back, sir. Make sure it gets nice and hot. Don't you worry, sir."

As the steward left, Pilot Tillman shook his head with a cringe.

"Them people," he said, then banged his hand against a side panel. "You can't count on them to figure nothin' out," he added in a low voice, swallowing hard.

Brady scowled, turning his head away. No doubt, after fifteen minutes of the man's rants, he had the pilot figured out.

"Pilot Tillman." He pushed out a deep breath. "I can't just stand here and listen to the way you talk to your black help. It's disgusting, and I can't be a part of it. I've got to get off this boat."

The window of the pilothouse door rattled as he slammed it shut behind him.

* * * * *

"Good to have you home, son. I've missed you—with your mother gone, and then you at your uncle's all that time. I was feeling pretty lonely."

Brady gazed up at his father. "Well, ending up at home is about the only thing that makes sense after all the messes I've been in. I can't believe it. I'm a failure as a newspaper abolitionist. I lost a whole load of food to river pirates. Then I finally get a chance at my dream job, and it's with a fellow who looks down on black people. No way could I work ten months with that guy!"

"Sounds to me like you need to spend more time with your God figuring out who you really are."

Brady cocked his head and swallowed. His father always had a way of grounding the discussion. "You're probably right, Father."

"Then in your spare time, you can help me get the crops out of the field." He spun to leave, chuckling to himself with an affirming nod. "We both benefit!"

One thing about his father—the closer he got to the black soil, whether in thought or deed, the more nuggets of wisdom he could unearth.

Chapter 16

Months later, Brady set the broom against the store-room wall in the general store near his father's home in St. Louis. He emptied the dustpan into the garbage bin. Before him, a stack of burlap bags of sugar and flour waited to be emptied into their display containers.

As if he didn't get enough dust sweeping the floor, filling the containers would leave more in the air. He'd had enough of the dust! He shuffled out of the storeroom.

Mr. Reese met him halfway. The old man's bushy gray eyebrows arched high over his wire-rimmed glasses.

"When you're done filling those containers, could you sweep the floor, Brady?"

"Oh, I just did, Mr. Reese." He pounded a fist against his thigh.

Mr. Reese removed his glasses and wiped them with his apron hem. "Well, my eyesight may be failing me, but how is it I can still see dirt in the corners?"

"Guess I must have missed some spots, sir." Brady's gaze darted from the near corner, past some balance scales on a back counter, to a far corner.

Mr. Reese frowned and shook his head, then placed his hands on his hips. "Your heart is just not in this anymore, is it?"

Brady released a heavy sigh. "Maybe that's it, sir. I can tell you where my head's at, though. It's filled with dust."

"For the first month, it was a whole different story. You did a great job. Maybe you need to find something to do outdoors. Didn't you say your uncle had a spot open up in the wood supply business? Taking care of all those steamboats?"

"Yeah, I've had experiences on those scows before. Didn't end up well. Once my head is clear, though, maybe I'll have a fresh perspective." He scrubbed a hand over his face.

* * * * *

Brady lay restless in bed that night. No sooner had he found peace with one thought, another darted into his head. His mind eventually wandered to the *Robinson Crusoe* book he so admired. He envisioned the scene late in the story when Crusoe dreamed about a man descending from a great black cloud like a bright flame of fire. He was carrying a spear. Crusoe was terrified and feared for his life.

Crusoe awoke from his frightening dream and became introspective, examining his life. He realized how sin had been such a part of his entire life and how helpless he was without God. Brady became introspective about his own life. Was not it the same in so many ways? Did not each sin need reconciliation? There were many--chasing after a black fugitive, offering money to a bounty hunter, leaving Mr. Lovejoy in the midst of his battle, leaving Charlotte in limbo.

And so it had been for Saul in the Bible, as he became the apostle Paul on the road to Damascus. Once the persecutor of Christians, Paul became a champion of spreading the light.

After a long night, Brady woke up the next morning surprisingly refreshed. He sprang out of bed.

* * * * *

Late that afternoon, Brady's father walked through the front door, perusing their mail. He paused at a slim white envelope. "There's one here for you, Brady. From that Elijah Lovejoy fellow."

Brady snatched it from his father's hand and ripped it open.

"I suppose he wants you back." His father poured two glasses of lemonade. They sat together at the kitchen table as Brady eagerly read the letter.

"You're right, Father. He's got a special project for me if I'll accept. Seems business is good and circulation is up." He read further. "Listen to this. He would like me to go to Cincinnati to personally escort a press back to Alton." Brady paused to whisper the two words personally escort back to himself. *My, they have a nice ring.* A rush of warmth filled his head.

"I can't imagine you wanting to interrupt your exciting life here just to do that!" His father took a large swig of his drink and brusquely banged the glass back to the table.

Brady stood and began to pace. "Just think. I'd be the one responsible for the safe passage of that fine piece of machinery." He imagined sitting atop the crate at each port, his musket at the ready, his eyes ever vigilant toward any mischievous behavior.

But then his imagination carried him back to another vision— sitting high atop a rock along the river with Char, vigilant toward life along the river—a hawk squawking above, the whistle of an oncoming steamboat, the swish of the water tumbling off its churning paddlewheels. *And what of Char?* He'd better focus on reading the rest of the letter.

"Mr. Lovejoy says Char has been spending a lot of time at their house watching after little Edward Payson. His wife, Celia Ann, has remained strong, despite a number of health problems." He read on. "But Char's sewing business has been going well when she has the time."

"That's nice. So when does Mr. Lovejoy want you to go on your little adventure?"

"Next week." Brady swilled the rest of his lemonade—downing it in one gulp.

* * * * *

On the steamboat leaving St. Louis, Brady knew that this part of his trip on the Mississippi River would be short-lived. In Cairo, he'd have to change boats for another heading up the Ohio River. As he gazed out over the railing of the main cabin level, he reacquainted himself with the landmarks. Foster's Point, coming up on the starboard side, had a sheer drop-off just past the point. The boat would be safe hugging the shoreline. He looked forward to see if the pilot would do just that.

He was also anxious to plan where to situate the press. Even though it would be coming back on a different boat, they were enough alike that he could make plans. Once the boat had hugged the cliff along Foster's Point, bringing a smile to his face, he headed down.

The main deck had an odd mixture of freight. On the larboard side, a pen held four noisy pigs, no doubt on their way to a slaughterhouse downstream. Their raucous squealing as he strode by told him they were disappointed he was not bringing food. Across from the pen were several crates. He imagined the press crate would look something like them, with roughhewn boards protecting unknown contents, visible only through cracks between the slats.

An open space in the distance seemed to be an ideal spot as it provided a good vantage point to view oncoming troublemakers.

Walking toward that spot, Brady passed other skids, then jolted back a step as a head poked out between two of them.

"Psst, Brady." The head appeared to be vaguely familiar, but Brady couldn't identify him.

"It's me, Samuel. Remember? Malcolm's brother."

Brady caught his breath and did a quick scan of his surroundings. Seeing no one else nearby, he bent between the crates, out of sight.

"Yeah, now I remember. What are you doing here?"

While no immediate answer came, his heart beat faster. *Am I being drawn into another fugitive slave fiasco?*

His raspy voice finally responded, "I'm a hopin' I can trust you."

"Well, I'm not so sure I'm your guy. What are you up to?" Brady held his breath as his brow pinched tight together.

"I'm runnin' away." Samuel squeezed his eyes shut as he leaned back.

Brady popped his leery head up above the crate to double-check for unwanted strangers. *Now what?*

He chewed on his inner cheek, then finally stammered, "Oh, of course. I should have guessed." He edged in farther and kneeled between the crates as Samuel moved back. Brady craned his neck. "Is Malcolm with you?"

"No, he's got good work. Besides, he's got a girl too." He smiled, revealing a chipped tooth.

How could Samuel smile right now? Brady frowned. "Is your master after you?"

"Yes suh. I saw him get on the boat." Samuel's eyes blinked rapidly.

"Criminy." Brady had no choice now. He squared his shoulders and took a deeper breath, already feeling lightheaded from the shallow ones he'd been taking. "We've got to hide you better till we get to Cairo. You've got to get off there."

"Cairo? Why's that?"

"Switch boats. You want to get to Ohio, not Louisiana."

"You can say that again! The land of liberty." Samuel looked off into the distance, his eyes gleaming.

"First, we've got to figure out something—a better place for you to hide." And if anyone knew these boats, Brady was the one. He rubbed his suddenly throbbing temples. "There's a closet up on the main cabin deck. Where they keep the brooms, mops, and supplies. That should work. Cleaning is all done for the day. You should be safe there. Tell me, what's your owner look like?"

"Tall, thin, kinda old. Gray hair, but not much left on top."

"OK, I'm going to see if the way is clear. Wait here till I come back and get you. I hope he's not like a lot of other men wearing a hat today."

About five minutes later, Brady returned with a large box.

"Here." He passed it to Samuel. "You carry this and follow me. You need to look like you're working for me. Don't worry—it's not too heavy."

"Yes suh. Whatever you say."

They marched up the stairs to the cabin level, then inconspicuously headed aft by the wheelhouse where Brady opened a closet door.

"Stay inside here until we get to Cairo. That's three more stops. Pay attention and listen. I'll try to come back and check on you then. Here, I'll take that box back with me. Doesn't look like you have much room in there." He swooped it from Samuel's arms. "One other thing. When it's time to get off the boat, be careful. Chances are your owner will be watching by the end of the gangplank."

Samuel stepped into the closet, and Brady closed the door behind him.

* * * * *

Samuel didn't much care for dark closets, especially if you were stuck inside one. For one thing, they were just too dark. Far better to be able to see the friends you were cozying up to. For another, they were crowded. On this occasion, he had to make company with mops, brooms, dustpans, and pails. Of course, that was really only in his imagination—he couldn't actually see them. No room to lie down, or even sit, for that matter. But the worst part was the odors. How is it the stuff that's supposed to clean is the stuff that has such a strong smell?

He hoped Brady had given him good instructions. Get off at the third stop. And now, after two stops, Samuel anxiously awaited the third. He could feel a slowing down of the vibration driving the paddlewheels rhythmic churn. *This must be the stop coming up.*

The closet door sprang open, and the sudden flash of outside light blinded him. All he could see was the outline of a short boy. After a few seconds, the boy's features became clearer. Slightly plump, he was a young white teen with a round face and short-shorn brown hair. His eyes bulged, and he took a step back— probably scared to see Samuel's big white eyes popping out from the dark.

"Don't be 'fraid, boy," Samuel said, taking a wary half-step out of the closet. "I'm just hidin'. I won't hurt you. I'm Samuel. What's your name?"

"David," came out softly. The boy's wary eyes seemed distant and unfocused.

"Don't worry. I'll be leavin' right quick. This must be Cairo, right?"

"No," he said after a slight delay while shaking his head.

"No? Then what stop is this?" Samuel scratched his cheek.

"Wood," the boy mouthed slowly.

"Ah." Samuel nodded. "I got it. Are we stoppin' for wood?"

David nodded his head up and down but said nothing more.

"Didn't we get loaded up with wood in the last big town?" Samuel asked with an uncertain tone.

"Pine." His eyes looked distant.

"Pine? What's you talkin' about, boy? Help me out here."

"Burns too fast." A gleam sparked in the boy's blue eyes.

"Oh, I think I'm followin' you now. When we picked up wood the last time, it was pine, and that burns too fast. We need hard-wood now. Is that it?"

David's head bobbed up and down with a big smile. He then reached for a mop and pail and set them outside the door. Turning around again facing Samuel, he put his hand on Samuel's chest and pushed him farther back into the closet.

David shut the door. The walls of total darkness closed in on Samuel again. He yelled out through the door, "Thank you, David. You's just like me—a child of God too."

Chapter 17

Brady peered out at the great brooding river stretching wide before him. The morning's heavy dampness had given way to a much lighter afternoon. His heart felt lighter, as well. Stops at Chester and Cape Girardeau and one more for wood had been short. Now he anxiously awaited the Cairo stop and transfer to another steamboat. He made his way to the closet where Samuel was hiding. He knocked softly on the door. No response.

Opening the door, he found nothing but brooms and mops. No Samuel! Brady hurried to the larboard side where he could view the gangplank being lowered on the level beneath him.

One of the first people off was a tall elderly man with a balding head—he must be Samuel's owner. But what had happened to the young man with the chipped tooth?

* * * * *

Brady kept trying to push the thought of Samuel away. He would board the Randolph and look forward to its departure up the Ohio River early in the morning.

Before dawn broke, he awoke with an urge to check out the main level storage. After all, this was most definitely a trip to secure a printing press for Mr. Lovejoy, not a dash to liberty by someone he barely knew. According to the schedule, this boat would turn around and carry the press for the return leg from Cincinnati. Brady now walked among the skids. Just as the day before, a low voice hailed him from between the crates.

Brady turned and whispered, "Samuel, is that you?"

"Yes suh, Brady. Followed you from a distance."

"How did you get off the other boat? I saw your owner watching for you."

"I ain't good at much. But I kin swim! Waited till dark to dive off the other side a the boat."

"Well, good for you. No wonder your clothes still look damp."

"Can't 'magine my master chasin' me more." A playful grin spread across his face.

"How's that?"

"I just ain't worth that much to him!"

* * * * *

Disembarking back toward home with the press from Cincinnati went smoothly. The wooden crate, surrounded by others on the Randolph's main deck, was totally inconspicuous.

Once underway, Brady headed up to get better views of the marvelous river, figuring the crate was only at risk during port stops. He now pondered the steps to the pilothouse. *Should I march right up to say hello?* He could act as if he were right at home there and make astute comments about the river, reading the current, offering intelligent conversation with the man in charge.

When he poked his head through the door, a young man, looking even a few years younger than him, was doing that very thing, not letting the interruption stop him.

Brady listened for a moment until the pilot finally turned and asked, "Can we help you? This is a private area, you know."

"Oh, just saying hello," Brady mumbled as his spirits sank low, and he hurried to leave, tripping on the step down.

* * * * *

During the stops at Louisville, Henderson, and now Cairo, Brady had sat atop the press crate with his musket in hand. The only attention he got was stares from several deckhands. One finally stopped to talk.

"Must be somethin' special," the middle-aged black man queried, no doubt hoping Brady would be in a talkative mood.

"Yes, it is," Brady responded. "I'm here to make sure nothing happens to it."

"Where's it going to?" He raised curly eyebrows.

"Alton, Illinois."

The man lifted his head higher and looked around. "I see. Won't you tell a fella what's inside? Makes me curious."

"All right. I guess it won't hurt telling you. It's a printing press."

"What's it for?"

"Prints newspapers."

"Oh, I can't read, so I wouldn't much care about it. Why'd anyone want to hurt it? What would they do to it, anyway?"

"People might want to throw it in the river. Presses have landed in the water before. Those people don't like what the newspaper says, and that's their foolish way to object. But it's meant to help people like you."

"Ya don't say! And the folks who want to throw it in the water—they's the people who can read? Blazes!"

"Well, I'd say a lot of them can't read newsprint, either. But they sure can read emotions on the faces of a rowdy crowd getting worked up all around them."

* * * * *

As deckhands secured the Randolph's moorings upon arrival in St. Louis, Brady took his vigilant spot atop the crate. Of all the towns, this one most worried him. Surely, some malcontents were still around from Mr. Lovejoy's days at the St. Louis Observer.

A great commotion could be heard a ways off as many people disembarked via the boarding ramp on the starboard side. Moments later, others came on board. Brady felt a bit isolated until three men approached.

"What are you doing guarding that crate, bud?" one asked as he drew closer.

Brady gripped the stock of his musket tighter.

"Wouldn't happen to be a printing press headed to Alton, would it? Let me see the writin' on the side." The man came closer, then circled around it.

Brady's eyes widened, but he kept them focused on the men in front of him.

"None of your business," he replied.

Then a sudden blow to his head from behind knocked him dizzy. Two of the men each grabbed an arm and yanked him off the crate, his musket flying.

Brady went crashing to the floor. He tried to get back up on a knee but a swift kick of a boot to his stomach left him breathless. His lungs gasped for air.

"Don't beat him up too bad, Bill. He's not much more than a kid."

"A kid whose thinking is way off kilter. Seems to me that head needs a good straightening out, if you ask me." He kicked at Brady's head, his boot coming away shining wet, blood on its tip. A continuous barrage of swinging legs and boots struck him. Brady feared his head would explode.

"Enough, Bill!" one of the others yelled, trying to pull him off.

Another kick, and once more. All went dark.

* * * * *

Charlotte sat with Mr. Lovejoy in the hospital room where Brady was kept. He lay still with his eyes closed. She blew her nose in her handkerchief, wishing that it would somehow take away the antiseptic smell as well. She stood up to pace but soon found herself collapsed back in her chair, her heartbeat now throbbing. *Why did I wait so long?* Now it took an event like this to reconnect them.

"I don't understand why he's still unconscious." She stared at Mr. Lovejoy. "If we can believe the report, it's been almost twenty-four hours since those thugs laid into him."

"Yeah, they really must have hit his head hard. But he's a tough fellow—resilient. He'll come around." His nervous clearing of his throat did not inspire confidence.

She released a deep sigh as she reached to smooth Brady's bedspread, the warmth seeping through from his body reassuring. "Right now I'm really feeling bad about how things fell apart between Brady and me."

Mr. Lovejoy moved closer, sitting down right beside her. "I must admit, I never took the time to talk to you about it. Do you care to tell me?"

She cast an appreciative smile back to him. That was so typical of Mr. Lovejoy—always concerned about others. "To answer your question, I guess there was a moment when I thought his heart wasn't really into freeing us black people."

"I know he was always very fond of you—that's for sure." He patted her on the knee.

"Yeah, I have felt that, no doubt. But he was never at ease around any of my friends or even my mama." She lowered her head and closed her eyes, remembering him squeezing out of her mama's hug.

"Maybe as a younger boy, he just never really had any black people in his life."

"Could be. Or might be because he keeps blaming Sandford for his mother's death. But that was so long ago."

"Well, maybe he's changing, and it just takes time. Looks like he's willing to put more than his heart and soul into our cause.

Now we see he's even thrown his body into it. Just look what he's gone through." He released a heavy sigh.

Chapter 18

The blurry visages of the two people staring at him were becoming clearer. His question, "Where am I?" prompted a response from Mr. Lovejoy.

"The hospital in St. Louis."

"You look a bit rough," Charlotte added with a half-smile while standing next to the bed and leaning over him. Brady hoped the smile part was because she was happy to see someone she still cared about.

"Your head looks like a big apple bruised all over," she continued, then chuckled. "No way would I take you home from the market."

"How did you find me?" He tried to sit up, but the pain in his stomach said no.

"Well, when the press didn't show up, we figured we'd better come down and look for you. Managed to just catch a steamboat coming this way."

"And the press?"

"I think you know." His boss touched Brady's arm, a sad glint in his eyes. "Another one in the river." His voice trailed off, his eyebrows pinching together.

Brady wanted his own eyes to go back out of focus. Oh, how he wished he didn't have to see the pain covering Mr. Lovejoy's face!

"I'm sorry, sir. I've let you down." His voice trembled slightly as he turned away, for the first time noticing other patients lying in beds across the room, scant light from a side window leaving some in shadows.

"Not all your fault, Brady. I've underestimated the resolve of the people we're up against. It all just makes me more determined. We'll get another press up to Alton one way or another."

A nurse came in and shoved a thermometer into Brady's mouth, then checked a bandage over his eye. A moment later, she said, "Temp is coming down near normal."

"Nurse, may I talk with you outside?" Mr. Lovejoy asked.

Once they had left, Charlotte spoke up. "It's been a long time, Brady."

"Yeah, since I last had any sort of connection with you." He took in a deep breath. "So, tell me. If you found that bruised apple in your satchel, would you throw it out?"

"Of course not. There'd be plenty of good apple underneath."

Brady's eyes welled up.

She reached for his hand and squeezed it. "I might be kinda hard on myself for not taking better care of it, though."

"That can apply to lots of things besides apples," he replied. "It's too bad more people don't think about what's underneath the surface."

"You don't have to tell *me* that!" She remained quiet for a moment. "I'm sorry, Brady," she continued. "I've been thinking about you a lot. I know you care more about me and my people than I gave you credit. I do realize for you it's more than just freedom of the press."

"I always hoped there was a future for you and me." His searching eyes focused on hers.

"I know there was a time we had something special." She pushed his bangs off to the side. A narrow shaft of light revealed a shiny dampness around her eyes.

Mr. Lovejoy returned to the room. "Good news," he said. "The nurse asked the doctor when you could get released. Does tomorrow sound soon enough?"

"Terrific," replied Charlotte, somehow beating Brady's words echoing the same thoughts.

"I hope I can walk out of here," he added with a snicker.

"I'm hoping you'll consider returning to Alton." Mr. Lovejoy placed a hand on Brady's sheet-covered knee, and as he stood there, the weight and warmth of his touch and words pulsed so far past the bruises. "The battle has a ways to go yet. God definitely needs a warrior with us like you, Brady. Please come back and join us."

* * * * *

Nationally, Mr. Lovejoy was obtaining increased popularity and stature. Local resistance to the Observer, however, remained strong. He went to his financial backers and offered to resign, but when a consensus opinion could not be reached, he remained editor. As a means of covering the cost of a new press, he made an appeal, through the help of the Alton Telegraph, to subscribers and others for financial help. The fifteen hundred dollars he needed soon came in, and he ordered another press.

"I'm going to need your help again, Brady," Mr. Lovejoy said upon arriving at the office one morning. "But this time, I won't ask you to be a guard—just be a watchman. Be vigilant on the boat so you can pull in others as needed. I've enlisted the help of a pilot named Carson, who previously had years of experience in law enforcement. On this end, I've convinced Mayor Krum to assign a constable to get the press from the boat, once at the wharf, to the safety of a locked warehouse."

"Sounds like a good plan," Brady responded. "I'd love to make another trip on a boat from Cincinnati. Besides, it's been a month, so all my former injuries have long been healed—it's a distant memory."

Mr. Lovejoy chuckled. "I just knew you couldn't say no."

"Maybe this time, if I run into trouble, I can somehow invoke the wrath of God."

"I'd rather we invoke God's love. At least that's what I teach in Sunday school all the time. We'd all be much better off living with more love."

Brady leaned back in his chair, his hands clasped behind his head. Amazing, he thought. *With all that's going on, that man still has time to teach Sunday school.*

* * * * *

The morning fog of mid-September had mostly lifted, but still lingered along some of the recesses of the Ohio River shoreline. A slight chill reminded Brady fall wasn't far away, although the leaves were fending off any takeover by gold and red hues.

Now, a new sense of optimism stole in with the morning mist. Safely loaded with a crate containing a new press, the Moselle disembarked from Cincinnati. Brady took the opportunity to talk with Pilot Carson shortly after departure. Mr. Lovejoy had sent a letter to Pilot Carson, with bonus money, outlining his wishes.

"I hope you don't mind my visiting with you, Pilot Carson. Just want to make sure we all know Mr. Lovejoy's expectations."

"Yes, I received Mr. Lovejoy's letter, and I'm prepared to step in when needed. But I need you to tell me when that should be."

"Understood. I plan to check on the crate frequently, but I'm not going to stay there full-time because I just draw undue attention." Brady stood silent, then asked, "Where's your cub pilot today?"

"A last-minute problem came up. I'm going to miss him. I wish I had him here because he's a gem."

"Well, just so you know, I've had a lot of experience. Not so much on the Ohio, but I know the Mississippi leg from Cairo to Alton like the back of my hand. I love piloting."

"Is that right? Good to know." Carson took a big swallow from his coffee mug.

Brady looked out at a passing scow loaded with wood. *I'd rather be on this boat than that one*, he thought as the two boats passed in opposite directions. The two men remained silent for several minutes.

"So that boss of yours—he's not afraid to speak his mind." Carson leaned in toward Brady. "Getting some national attention, isn't he?"

"That's for sure." A hawk sweeping down toward the boat distracted him. "But a strong core of dissidents are fighting him. This is the third press he's had to order in little over a year."

"Gosh, that's something. I believe he should have the right to print what he wants. I just don't think the country is ready for abolition, though."

"Well, unfortunately, that's how a lot of people especially down here feel." An upcoming point caught Brady's attention. "Say, I'd better jot down some notes." He grabbed his notebook off the front panel. "Didn't realize that reef was so prominent." After a few quick notes, he returned the notebook.

"Getting back to Mr. Lovejoy," Brady continued, "I sure do admire how fiercely he's staked out his position." He remained quiet a moment, then ventured a probing question. "How do you feel about the problem?"

"Well, I like the compromise of colonization—free all those folks but let them go back to Africa where they came from. Wouldn't they be happier there than working as slaves?"

"Several years ago, believe it or not, that's where Mr. Lovejoy was at. But his faith has led him to believe full equality and rights is the only answer, and God has ordained him to help bring that about."

"Very courageous. I tip my hat to him." Pilot Carson reached for his cap and tipped it.

Brady stared out the side window as the boat hugged the shoreline. A fish jumped from the water and shook itself in midair as if to bask in a moment of God-given freedom, then fell back into the water with a huge splash.

"I guess I'd better get down to check the crate."

* * * * *

As the day grew long, Brady made multiple forays three levels down to the main level where all the crates were stored. Unlike his earlier trip a month ago, he kept his distance, watching for any suspicious activity.

When not watching the crate, Brady made a point of visiting with Mr. Carson, sharing his observations about rocks now appearing with lower water levels, the changing shoreline, and sandbars. He was beginning to feel more comfortable with the Ohio River stretch, as this was now his third trip. But as darkness enveloped them, he felt lost. Occasional buoys with lanterns atop them were welcome sights. It was well into the night before they docked in Cairo. Brady slept well, knowing further travel would await morning.

The next day, he forewarned Pilot Carson about his concerns with St. Louis, where they would arrive come evening. He recounted the story of his attack a month earlier. Throughout the day, he found himself rubbing the back of his neck, closing his eyes, and taking calming breaths. Far better to focus on something familiar along the shoreline—a prominent rock serving as a resting spot for a gull. He gulped down dinner, oblivious to what he actually had eaten, and headed down to find a good vantage point from which to spy on the crate.

Once the Moselle had docked in St. Louis, Brady carefully watched each person who walked among the wooden crates. A couple of the large boxes were transported off the steamboat, but the press remained untouched. He released a sigh of relief when two deckhands stood abreast of the gangplank preparing to lift it prior to departure.

But at the last moment, four men rushed aboard. Brady peered intently. *Can I recognize any of them?* Not in the fading light of early evening. He moved a bit closer, hiding behind another crate. They walked among several of the big boxes, their backs to him. Then one turned around. He was the one who had beat him up before! But what were their plans? They'd missed their opportunity as the boat was already disembarking.

"I'll look for a wheeled cart," one of them said, just barely audible over the engine noise.

Knowing he'd better alert Pilot Carson, Brady rushed back up to the pilothouse.

"We've got trouble." He flung open the door and gripped the handle tight to steady his headlong run. "Some bad-looking fellows are eyeing the press crate." He bent over, bracing his hands on his knees as he drew in heavy breaths.

"Oh yeah? How many?" Pilot Carson bit down on his bottom lip.

"Four, including one I recognize from the earlier incident." Still gulping air, he was able to stand up straight now.

Pilot Carson lifted his cap and ran a hand through his hair. "Do you think they're going to try to push it over along the way?"

"Maybe. Not sure. I always thought they wanted to do it where it would get the most attention afterward—you know, like in a port. But in the end, they just want to keep Mr. Lovejoy from printing." Brady felt his leg muscles tightening, his knees starting to lock.

"Maybe they're waiting until Alton. We've got a bit less than an hour to go." Pilot Carson looked through all sides of the windows, double-checking his bearings. "I'd better go down and find out exactly what's going on." He paused a moment and cleared his throat. "Well, Pilot Scott. You said you knew this part of the river. Are you ready to take over?"

"Without a doubt!" As warmth filled his chest, his cheeks flushed. He offered a crisp salute as he stood a bit taller.

"All right! I've got to first round up my firearm. Stay close to the speaking tube. Once I get situated, I'll try to get in touch from down below." The way Pilot Carson set his jaw gave Brady goose bumps.

"Cast your worries aside, sir!" Brady stepped to the wheel and grasped it with a firm grip. He peered ahead into the fading evening light. "Yep," he said, his tense muscles now relaxing. "That's Watson's Point over there." With a satisfied smile, he added, "We're going wide."

Chapter 19

Brady kept looking over to the speaking tube, waiting for it to live up to its name. Where was Mr. Carson? What was taking him so long? Maybe it was just his own ears. Could it be they were failing him at this critical time?

Finally, the sound of his voice came through.

"Brady, can you hear me?" Pilot Carson sounded out of breath.

"Yes sir. I was beginning to get worried."

"Sorry it took so long. I've got the four guys right here in front of me. I made a few stops first. Pilot Abrams was sound asleep for the early morning shift. I let Captain Francis know what we were up to. He agreed with our plan. I had to tell him you were an expert cub pilot, well schooled in this part of the river. None better!"

"Thank you, sir." Brady's heart throbbed as he planted his feet wide.

"Please don't let me down," came back loud and clear through the tube.

"Don't worry, sir." He leaned forward, looking ahead to make sure he was on track.

"So where was the press crate when you last saw it?"

"Near the center, forward of the engines." His pulse increased.

"Ah, these blokes have already managed to move it all the way to the starboard gunwale. Don't know if they could lift it over, but I'm glad I caught them when I did."

"You bet. So, are those ruffians cooperating?"

"Once in a while, they get a little feisty, and I have to show them who's boss. The barrel of my musket is always a good persuader. Of course, they keep saying they haven't committed any crime."

"Yet," Brady was quick to add.

"You're right." A moment of silence followed.

It was broken by a loud bang at the front of the boat. The banging continued several times until reaching the transom.

Brady winced as, at first, the noise was startling to his jumpy nerves. His heartbeat soon settled, though, as he recognized the sound. It should not be new to an experienced cub pilot.

"I suspect that was a log floater," Brady offered.

"Your suspicion is no doubt correct—you've probably run into one of those before. Don't worry. May have scuffed up the paint all along the hull, but doubt there are any holes."

"At least we better hope so, sir." A quiet lingered in the speaking tube, and Brady held his breath.

"Let me see. What time is it?" Pilot Carson started up again. "We've still got about twenty-five minutes before we arrive at Alton. I don't want to risk bringing these hoodlums up to the confines of the pilothouse. Heaven forbid."

The tube went quiet again. Then came, "Brady, have you ever docked a big boat like this?"

"Once, but it was in full daylight."

"I see. Would you feel comfortable doing it at night? If not, I can go roust Abrams up."

Brady struggled to find the words as he tried to picture himself bringing the large whale to rest at the Alton wharf. Darkness was already beginning to assert its hold on his surroundings. It would soon be ironclad.

"I-I feel good about i-it," he finally stammered. "It would help if there was more light, though."

"I can have one of the deckhands put up some more lanterns on the docking side. It's a good thing we're going upstream. As long as you cut the speed way down, there's little risk of overshooting the dock. You're going to have to use your engine bells to let the engineers on each side know what to do."

"Yes, I know just where those engine bell pullcords are—right here above me."

"I'm also going to try to get a clear view of the shoreline and dock from here so I can warn you if you get off track. Got to get another crate moved out of the way first."

Brady double-checked his own view, wiping with a cloth to remove any glare on the front glass.

"Hey," Pilot Carson continued with a chuckle, "I think I've got four guys here who have already figured out just how to move crates!"

With the pilot's lighthearted comment, a sense of relief calmed Brady's body. Before him, darkness had settled in. He tried to locate the moon and was happy to find the three-quarter-full beacon lighting the way. Its radiance shimmered off the waters, quiet but for the boat's bow plunging headlong in front of him. About twenty minutes later, as he steered around a bend, a slight glow from the town's lights made it through the nighttime mist. Just ahead on the right, a familiar dock soon appeared.

A minute later came Pilot Carson's steady voice. "We're slowin' her way down now. Pull her down."

Brady's pulse seemed to race in contrast with the slowing steamboat.

"Start your starboard turn."

His heart now pounded in his chest. *The rate of turn is the most critical thing.*

"Easy now. A bit more. More I said . . . more! What are you waiting for? You're not turning enough! Wait! Shut down the starboard engine. Ring the bell. Ring it!"

Brady rang the stopping bell so the engineer would close the throttle valve to the starboard engine.

"Okay, let the current push us back a bit. Now move back in. Start up the starboard engine."

Brady rang the bell. They moved forward again, and he steered a more aggressive turn.

"That's right. Turn it. Nice, you're on track. That's it. You've got it."

A solid bump caused him to lurch slightly to the side.

"Good job. Now two long whistles and one short," Pilot Carson said with a heavy sigh of relief.

Brady pushed a foot pedal to actuate the whistle two long blasts and one short to announce their landing.

"Tie her up, mates, tie her up," Pilot Carson's voice boomed. Then in a softer tone, he directed his comments through the speaking tube to Brady. "You adjusted well, son. Congratulations."

"Thank you, dear Lord," Brady whispered to himself, a sense of peace permeating his body.

* * * * *

A flash of light caught Brady's eye. Peering from the first deck out upon a throng of people greeting the Moselle, he saw lantern light reflect off the constable's shiny badge. Brady's eyes moved up to a dimly lit mustached face. Yes, it was Constable Morgan—here as planned to safeguard the passage of the press to a warehouse. Brady exhaled his relief.

Several minutes later, he was on shore greeting Constable Morgan with a hearty handshake. "I'm so glad to see you here, Constable." Brady smiled for the first time all evening.

"Well, Mr. Lovejoy impressed upon me the importance of all of this. He also sent some people here to help transport the press to the warehouse. We're planning to post a guard until midnight, as well."

"Wonderful. You should know there were some characters on the boat with bad intentions. Pilot Carson kept them at bay, so we can't say they actually committed a crime."

* * * * *

The following morning, Mr. Lovejoy had asked Charlotte to go check on the press at the warehouse. He had decided to spend the morning at home, helping Celia Ann, pregnant with their second child.

Finding the warehouse door ajar, with no press inside, Charlotte raced with her fears down to the wharf. She dreaded that those fears might get there first. Off the end of the pier, a lonely gull rested upon a piece of metal protruding from the water's surface. A pain radiated in her stomach like someone had punched her. She couldn't breathe. Surrounded by fresh air, yet she couldn't pull it in! Tears flowed down her cheeks, lingering with a biting saltiness on the tips of her lips.

"Oh, Mr. Lovejoy," she mouthed in pain. "I am so sorry. I am so, so sorry . . . "

The gull scanned the waters ahead and then seemed to be looking back at her—most oblivious to her emotions. Why was he there? For new explorations, new adventures, new opportunities? Some simple words, in poetic cadence, started to form in her head.

A most unusual spot,
But, lo, he knows it not.
A fresh new resting place
In this wide-open space.

His latest vantage point,
But little does he care,
The heartbreak it causes
If he only knew where.

For adventures await,
He must scope them all out.

But, no, that is not yours!
Surely, *that* can't I shout?

Charlotte could manage but a whimper. She wept in soft faint gasps. Like a bird, could she somehow look at this as something new? She most certainly could not feel that now. But ever? Was God still to deliver some new opportunity?

Chapter 20

Mr. Lovejoy was so distraught by the drowning of his third press into the Mississippi River, he decided he must get away from Alton with his family. He took them to Celia Ann's mother's home some distance away in St. Charles, Missouri.

While there, he had the opportunity to preach sermons at Reverend William Campbell's church for both morning and evening services. That night, on the way out of church, a stranger approached him discreetly with a note.

Elijah was troubled to read: "Mr. Lovejoy, be watchful as you come from the church tonight." It was signed, "A friend." But he proceeded on, inviting Rev. Campbell as their guest.

Nothing transpired on the way home, and Elijah thought no more of the matter until later. Around ten o'clock, as Rev. Campbell, Mrs. Lovejoy, their sick child, her mother and sister, along with Elijah, were occupying rooms upstairs; a loud knocking on the front door interrupted them.

"Who's there?" Mrs. Lovejoy yelled out in a shrill voice.

"We want to see Mr. Lovejoy. Is he in?" came the gruff reply.

"Yes, I am here," Elijah shouted as he rocked out of his chair and cast a darting glance at the clock.

The noise of the unlocked door creaking open alarmed them. Then the footsteps of two men marching upstairs broke the silence. The men barged into the room where Elijah stood, grabbed him, and tried to pull him downstairs. When he resisted, they beat him with their fists. He was dragged down to the front porch where a mob of angry men awaited. *Was this the prelude to being tar and feathered?*

Fists began to strike him as a throng of people cheered on. Mrs. Lovejoy soon joined the fracas and tried to force her way through the crowd, but was rudely pushed back. One man pulled a knife, at which point Celia Ann struck him in the face and proceeded on to find Elijah, wrapping her arms around him with a protective hug. Elijah's fear was momentarily replaced by one of amazement and pride in her fortitude. As attackers cursed, she continued to fend off the "mobites," as they were called, with strikes to their faces.

"You must take me before you take my husband," she proclaimed. Her unfailing devotion would leave more of a mark on Elijah than his beatings.

Eventually, their efforts, aided by her mother and sister, caused the mobites to give up and depart. Physically and emotionally exhausted, Mrs. Lovejoy fainted. When she recovered, Elijah brought her to a bedroom upstairs, where she lay distraught, often crying out hysterically.

"I'm very alarmed over her condition," Elijah confided to her mother, "especially since she's several months along with our precious second child. Not to mention what sick little Edward has had to go through." With a grimace, he tried to rub the tense muscles at the back of his neck.

But the mob returned a second time and marched back upstairs to the bedroom. Oblivious to Mrs. Lovejoy's fragile condition, they lurched out to seize Elijah again.

"You must stop this ungodly work of the devil!" Rev. Campbell boldly asserted. "You cannot go to church one day, and then do the likes of this. Jesus must be weeping in heaven." His words did manage to calm them and convince them to leave.

Rev. Campbell's efforts were short-lived, however, as the mob returned a third time. On this occasion, Mr. Lovejoy felt he had no other choice but to negotiate.

"I will provide you," he said, "a written, signed letter stating I will leave Missouri and return to Illinois." His promise appeased the mobites for the night.

Early in the morning, before the sun had risen, Elijah snuck out of the St. Charles house and returned to Alton. Upon arrival, he was alarmed to run into a man who claimed, "I helped destroy your press in Alton." Alerting his friends of ongoing danger even in Alton, Mr. Lovejoy was able to round up about ten armed people to help safeguard his house.

* * * * *

Brady stood with Charlotte in the store perusing books on a shelf.

"Isn't it amazing that books are now becoming more available to us?" she commented.

"Yeah, publishing has really improved over the last few years. Why, I've heard there's actually something such as a cookbook."

"Really?"

"Wouldn't you know, here is one." He pulled a book from the shelf and handed it to her.

"Say," he resumed, "didn't you mention your mother has a birthday coming up?"

"Yes, October 27. I'm looking forward to it. She always likes to celebrate in some small way."

"I'd like to buy her a gift, and I was thinking of a book." He leaned in toward Charlotte with a smile.

"Brady, it's sweet that you want to buy her something, but a book may not be the best thing." She smiled and tilted her head. "Don't you know, Mama can't read."

"Oh, I know. But you've got to start somewhere. With a simple book of recipes, we could teach her all about the important words." He grabbed the cookbook from her hands and began to flip through it.

"What do you mean by important words? You mean like *sugar*?" She released a smattering of a laugh.

"Exactly! I'm glad you mentioned the most important one."

"I think you might have some other motives in mind. Could it be you're looking for a change from chitlins and collard greens?" Her probing eyes left him a bit ill at ease—kind of like how he felt the day he had such a dinner over at her mama's house.

"All right, you know me all too well." He flipped through more pages to peruse the book in his hand. "This looks pretty simple. Looks like it has some tasty dishes in it."

"OK . . . maybe." She paused as she tilted her head to scan the shelf. "Say, I see one here that might interest you." She snatched *Explorers of the Mississippi River* and handed it to him.

"Hey," his voice rose, "I'll have to take a gander at this one." He flipped through a few pages. "Interesting. I'd like to look at this a bit longer. Why don't you go buy the recipe book, and I'll be along in a bit. But I insist on paying for it, so here's some money." He handed over some coins.

A few minutes later, concluding the river book was too expensive, Brady headed to the front of the store. Charlotte was standing there with the recipe book still in her hand.

"The other book was too much for too little new information. I already know a lot about it." The book and coins still in her hand caught his eye. "So why haven't you paid for that one yet?"

"Well, I tried to get the lady's attention, but she's been ignoring me."

"Can I help you, sir?" The older lady looked up over the rim of her thick glasses.

"Well, this young lady has been waiting here ahead of me," Brady said through clenched teeth.

"Oh, I figured she wouldn't have the money." The lady's forced smile seemed more of a smirk.

"Well then, we would like to buy this book she's been holding. She's got the money right here in her hands."

"We?" The lady fumbled the money as Charlotte handed it to her.

"Yes, we're buying this *together*." Brady put his arm around Charlotte's shoulder.

"Together? You two are together? Landsakes. I've seen everything." Her head kept shaking back and forth even as she handed back change. Brady reckoned it didn't stop until she lay her head on the pillow that night.

* * * * *

Earlier in the summer, Mr. Lovejoy had put out notice that he was planning a statewide antislavery convention to be held in Alton late in October.

Some of his friends thought he should be more inclusive of other viewpoints so a compromise of sorts could be thoroughly discussed and recommended. The concept of freedom of the press should be stressed, they said, and colonization might still be a possibility.

"Keep your interruptions to a minimum today," Mr. Lovejoy said as he came bouncing into the office this late-October morning. "I've got to concentrate on writing my speech for the convention."

Brady looked over at Charlotte with a knowing smile.

"That's fine," he said. "We're busy too. I've been working on the details of getting another press here by the end of October."

"I appreciate your running with that project for me and sending out the appropriate letters."

"Yeah, I've got a purchase agreement going to the printing press company and a letter to law enforcement folks in Cincinnati. We're asking the price of sending an actual lawman to accompany the press."

"What about space in Winthrop Gillman's warehouse? He told me earlier he would help us."

"I've got him to confirm he'd provide space to store the press when it comes. This time it will be way up on the third floor—should be safe there."

"I would think so." Mr. Lovejoy rubbed his furrowed forehead.

Hours later, Mr. Lovejoy came out of the office, paper in hand.

"I want to run some of what I've written by you both. You know how, after all these years, I value your opinions. Let me know what you think." He handed the papers to Brady.

Brady read down the page of the speech directed to the chairman of the convention. Certain paragraphs stood out to him. He shook his head in amazement. "I've got to read some of these paragraphs out loud to you, Char." He cleared his throat and began:

"I know that I have the right freely to speak and publish my sentiments. This right was given me by my Maker, and is solemnly guaranteed to me by the Constitution of the United States and of this state. What I wish to know of you is whether you will protect me in the exercise of this right, or whether I am to continue to be subjected to personal indignity and outrage."

Brady released an appreciative sigh and continued reading select parts out loud:

> *My rights have been shamefully, wickedly outraged; this I know and feel, and can never forget. But I can and do freely forgive those who have done it. . . . God in his providence—so say all my brethren, and so I think—has devolved upon me the responsibility of maintaining my ground here; and I am determined to do it. . . . A voice comes to me . . . calling upon me in the name of all that is dear in heaven or earth, to stand fast; and by the help of God, I will stand. . . . Sir, the very act of retreating will embolden the mob to follow me wherever I go. No sir, there is no way to escape the mob, but to abandon the path of*

duty. And that, God helping me, I will never do. . . . I appeal to every individual present. Whom of you have I injured? If any, let him rise here and testify against me. . . . And now you come together for the purpose of driving out a confessedly innocent man, for no cause but that he dares to think and speak as his conscience and his God dictate. Will conduct like this stand the scrutiny of your country? Of posterity? . . . Yet think not that I am unhappy. Think not that I regret the choice that I have made. While all around me is violence and tumult, all is peace within. . . . The rewarding smile of God is full recompense for all I forgo and all that I endure. Yes sir, I enjoy a peace which nothing can destroy. . . . I am commanded to forsake father and mother and wife and children for Jesus' sake, and as his professed disciple, I stand prepared to do it. . . . Before God and you all, I here pledge myself to continue—if need be, till death! "

Char's soft weeping, her head buried in her arms splayed across her desk, filled the room. Brady wiped tears from his own cheeks and draped a comforting arm around her shoulders. He looked back to see Mr. Lovejoy's eyes now wet with emotion but gleaming bright with resolve.

* * * * *

Close to three o'clock on an early-November morning, the Missouri Fulton approached the Alton wharf. Aboard the steamboat was the fourth press Mr. Lovejoy had ordered. As planned, this crate was well guarded. Brady joined a number of volunteers who helped transport the heavy crate from the dock to safe storage at Mr. Gillman's warehouse built of sturdy brick. Lifting the crate was a challenge, but with enough volunteers, they completed the task.

As morning broke, Brady felt relieved all seemed peaceful. Mr. Lovejoy went home. But others came to the warehouse with reports of pockets of unrest in the community.

So as not to repeat the mistake with the previous press, a group of volunteers was to be deployed to guard the press overnight. Brady volunteered with seventeen other men. He felt encouraged to have Mr. Gillman, himself—the building's owner—as one of those men.

Chapter 21

Only some of their eyes betrayed a mounting inner fear. Brady figured his surely did, if the pounding in his chest was any sign. The clamor outside penetrating the warehouse's thick brick walls had subsided. Brady now took stock of his fellow defenders. Dim candlelight revealed a reassuring arm draped over Mr. Lovejoy's shoulders as his head bobbed up and down in agreement. Others sat on nearby crates and barrels and fidgeted with their guns, cocking them or stroking their steel barrels, surely cold from the chill November air. But the question of the hour was would those barrels soon warm up? Brady flexed his fingers, loosening his tight grip from his musket.

The sound of clomping footsteps below reached them. Some of the fearful eyes now looked up toward a far door, likely imagining the men a floor below lumbering up the stairs. One set of steps was heavy and authoritative. The two following sounded lighter but dragged as if reluctant participants. The din outside had quieted—probably in anticipation of what was to follow from this meeting on the warehouse's third floor.

Just minutes ago, the noise had made Brady's ears throb. Brick and stones from the cobblestone street shattered the glass windows—most likely all of them. Shouts and taunts rumbled until indistinguishable one from another. An occasional gunshot had been fired from both sides, but were they aimed or were they mere shots in the dark?

The three men's gaunt visages now appeared through the doorway. Even in the dim light, Brady immediately recognized

Mayor Krum. He wasn't sure who the others were. Mr. Lovejoy stepped toward the approaching figures.

"Mayor Krum—I'm so glad to see you here." A long exhale followed as he extended his right hand to shake. "This is all spiraling out of control." A quick swipe across his brow flattened the furrows but revealed an unmistakable tremble to his hand.

After a deep breath raised his shoulders, Mr. Lovejoy continued, "We've got every right to defend ourselves and our property, do we not?" His voice, no doubt meant to sound assertive, cracked along the way.

"Yes, indeed you do," the mayor responded. "But somebody fired a shot that hit young Lyman Bishop."

"Oh my! Is he OK?" Elijah's eyebrows lifted in genuine concern.

"I believe he's going to be all right, but we can't let this escalate to something worse." A grimace flattened the mayor's mouth as he looked down, shaking his head side to side.

"Well, do you understand, my dear mayor, what this printing press represents?" Mr. Lovejoy filled his lungs with another deep breath. "If something ever stood for freedom of the press, this is it." His hand slammed down hard on one of the crates next to him.

"We are prepared," he continued, then grimaced with emotion. "We are prepared to defend it at all costs."

Brady's knees felt weak as he scanned the eyes of the other comrades, their worried gazes darting in every direction. *What does defend really mean?* Or was this small band of defenders just making time? They had no plan. They were not prepared. Yes, all but one of them had guns, but ten times as many people had gathered outside those brick walls.

The bells tolling from the nearby Presbyterian church tower joined his chorus of thoughts. With each toll, a sense of foreboding increased.

"Let's wait this out a bit." The mayor tilted his head back, thrusting his strong chin into profile. "Maybe things will settle down."

But the noise outside now increased. Folks appeared to be getting restless, having waited for the mayor to defuse the situation. Brady moved toward a window to survey the agitated crowd. The light from multiple torches illuminated angry faces. He recognized a familiar one near the building—that of Solomon Morgan—egging on the others. His staggering gestures and slurred speech were emboldened by a friendship he must have made earlier in the evening—with a bottle of liquor, probably now lying empty on a table in some bar. No doubt, more than a few in the crowd were feeling equally uninhibited. Brady looked for others he might recognize, but handkerchiefs covered their faces. He had a hunch, though, that some were his neighbors.

"Bishop is dead!" came the piercing shout from one reveler.

Brady slumped and turned back to relay the news. Was the shock on their faces from sympathy, or was it from outright fear?

Brady gazed out again at the crowd. Out of the corner of his eye, he spotted a man with a ladder. He was lugging it toward the windowless side of the building. *What was he up to?*

"I'll go talk to them." Mayor Krum hustled past the group, his tread heavy as he hastened downstairs.

Thud. Thud. Thud. Brady felt each step shaking something deep inside him. He tightened his sweaty grip on his musket. Would they listen to the man?

The door squeaked as the mayor opened it. Then his strident voice cut through the murmurs, encouraging the horde to settle down. Rioting was dangerous, he warned, and people would be prosecuted if they broke the law.

Brady touched the chilly glass pane—probably one of the building's only unbroken windows—and held his breath. What was happening down there?

Stepping in close, he rested his forehead against the window as he tipped his head to best see the reaction below.

"Get out of the way and go home!" someone yelled.

Bam!

Brady slammed his forehead against the glass while jumping at the exploding shot. More successive shots fired into the air.

He rubbed the bruised spot. Then his hand froze in place, every bit of him shivering.

He lurched from the window toward his fellow defenders. "Mr. Lovejoy. I saw them carrying a ladder to the side of the building," Brady said. "They had torches, too. What are they up to?"

Mr. Gillman must have heard him and rushed over. His face was ashen white. "You know," he said. "The roof is made of wood! They must be trying to set it on fire." He hunched over, his head drooping, as a new chant confirming those suspicions rose on the breeze.

"Burn them out. Burn them out. Burn them out!"

First one voice, then another, then dozens all crying the same thing.

"Burn . . . them . . . "

"Out."

"Burn. Burn. Burn!"

Brady wasn't sure if the words were still rising or just echoing in his head as his worst fears became real.

Elijah Lovejoy strode forward with gritted teeth. "No way— we can't let them burn the place. Who will join me to push that ladder down?" With uplifted arms, he exhorted his supporters.

"I will," said one middle-aged man in the back.

"Me too," a brash young man added.

"You'd better disguise yourself with handkerchiefs," Brady said, and once Elijah had nodded, Brady began to wrap one around the publisher's ruddy cheeks. Brady lingered and just stared as the two volunteers headed down the stairs with Elijah. *What bravery*, he thought.

Brady rushed to the window. He couldn't spot the ladder, but a glow of light from torches seeped around the side.

About ten minutes later, Elijah returned with the other men. He sighed and exhaled loudly with a fist raised high.

"Success!" he shouted. "We pushed the ladder over. Good work, fellas." He glanced back toward those who had helped him. "Must have been a friend or two down there, too. Someone in the crowd was willing to help us out. He tried to stop the kid on the ladder with the torch. I wonder if the ladder was tall enough anyway—to reach the top, that is."

"But what's next?" queried one of the other fellows. "This is all getting so out of control, Mr. Lovejoy. Don't you think they're just going to keep trying? We really have no choice but to surrender the press."

"We must fight it out." Mr. Lovejoy raised his fist again. "If necessary, to the bitter end. I, for one, am willing and ready to lay down my life!"

Brady's heart sank as his gaze darted around to the other fellows. He tried to gather his thoughts. *Were they in a warehouse or a mausoleum? How had he ended up here anyway?* He was hardly one to champion a cause. Mr. Lovejoy was no rabble-rouser either. But he did have his principles, including the right of a free press to support the abolition of slavery.

Brady wondered about the others. To his right was Mr. Gilman, the highly respected merchant, who owned the very building under attack. How his heart must ache with each shattered window. Across from him was Mr. Weller, who owned a store where many in the mob had probably bought their shoes. Surely, no one in the small group had imagined the night would turn out like this. And what about that crowd outside? *Some were probably just spectators curious about all the ruckus, weren't they?*

A mouse skittered across the floor and hid behind a crate. For a moment, Brady felt more like that mouse than a crusader for the abolition movement. In the distance, the church bells continued to toll. But a new intensity of shouts from the crowd drowned them out. Brady dashed back to the window.

"Burn them out! Shoot the abolitionists!" came the hysterical chants at a rising pitch.

Several of the men below were now tying two ladders together. They then headed back to the side of the building.

"They're going to try to light the roof on fire again," Brady yelled out.

Mr. Lovejoy stepped forward and rallied his group once more. "Who's going to go back down with me to knock that ladder over? Come on!"

Brady didn't know quite what to think, but he could no longer be just an observer. He volunteered along with Mr. Weller. The three of them bounded down the stairs. As they rushed into the open to push the ladder over, several shots rang out from behind a nearby woodpile. Mr. Weller grabbed his leg and stumbled. Mr. Lovejoy collapsed to the ground.

"I've been shot!" Elijah cried out. Brady and the wounded Weller reached for Mr. Lovejoy and managed to drag him back into the warehouse to the foot of the stairs.

Rev. Thurlbut came out of nowhere to assist. After a quick check, he said, "Elijah's got multiple wounds! This looks really serious." The reverend held his rifle tight and stood guard over him. Soon the other defenders came barreling down the stairs and looked with wide eyes and gawking mouths at the fallen Lovejoy. They fled, scattered gunfire at their backs.

As Brady now kneeled down near Elijah, several people entered the building. A man emerged from the shadows. His muffled voice sounded familiar when he asked, "Brady, are you OK?"

No, that's not my uncle! Is it? Can't be. Part of the mob? The man lowered his handkerchief. Brady's gaping mouth fell all the way open. He struggled to get the words out past the lump in his throat. "Uncle Raymond? I can't believe that's you!" he wailed. He swiped the back of his hand across his sweaty brow and looked away from something that at that moment was unfathomable.

"Oh, this is bad. This is really bad!" Brady cried out, his head trembling. He couldn't make it stop.

Chapter 22

Well past midnight, Brady sulked through the front door of his uncle's home. He had trudged back and forth through the streets of Alton for over two hours, muttering to himself, his head in a daze. The double blow of losing his dear friend and mentor, Elijah Lovejoy, then realizing his uncle was part of the mob absolutely crushed him. He couldn't possibly fathom feeling any worse.

Light came through the opening to the kitchen. He charged around the corner where his uncle and aunt were seated at the kitchen table, apparently waiting for him.

"You know he's dead," Brady shouted out, hoping his curt reaffirmation would carry plenty of extra guilt with it. "You must have seen that from your vantage point." Unable to look his uncle in the eye, he glared at one of his aunt's braided rugs beneath the dining room table, knowing full well his own eyes must be puffy and red.

"Yes, I know," came the solemn response of his uncle, also unable to meet Brady's eyes as silence took over the room and the painful moment seemed much too long.

"How could you?" Brady burst out screaming with an arm gesture sweeping high.

"I had no part in the shooting," his uncle mumbled. "Had no idea that was going to happen." He held his head between his hands, his elbows planted on the table.

"Then why were you there?" Brady's strong but shaky voice came back. "You couldn't stop what happened, even with a gun in your hand."

"Well, I knew you were with Lovejoy. Somehow I thought maybe I should be there in case you needed protection."

"That's true." Aunt Shirley's soft voice seemed to carry all the care she'd obviously put into the rug beneath her. "He was muttering your name when he left the house."

Silence followed as Brady stood staring at the floor.

"Mobs are terrible things!" he cried out. "Absolutely terrible."

"You add people pickled with liquor, and it becomes doubly bad." The shadow of his uncle's head shook back and forth across the rug. "First, there was that McIntosh fellow, and now Elijah. What has this country become?"

"I don't know how you're going to be able to live with this, Uncle Raymond." Finally, Brady looked up, his steady gaze piercing the man who had sheltered him for months. "I realize you may have been concerned about me, but if a person puts himself in a mob, he's going to have to own it."

"I think it will own me." Uncle Raymond returned his gaze with a less steady one, tears shining at its edges. "For the rest of my life."

* * * * *

The following day, Brady sat with Charlotte on the steps leading to the funeral director's home. Celia Ann and Elijah's two brothers, John and Owen, were inside making plans. They had indicated they would try to arrange to have the ceremony the next day—Elijah's birthday.

"I can't believe Elijah was only thirty-five," Charlotte mourned, her voice fading.

"Think of what all Elijah accomplished," Brady said, followed by a slight smile. "Funny thing—we always used to say Mr. Lovejoy. Now we both refer to him as Elijah."

"I feel closer to him that way," Charlotte responded. "Elijah is so much more endearing now, don't you think?" She leaned in toward Brady. "Since he's gone, I have this craving to feel closer to him. I suppose that happens most times a loved one dies."

"You're right. I'll always think of him now as Elijah." He nudged her shoulder with his. "Just like I always call you Char instead of Charlotte—it makes me feel a step closer to you."

At that, Charlotte's eyebrows bunched together, and she began crying, tears trickling down her cheeks.

Brady pulled her up from the step and hugged her tight. Releasing her, he wiped away some tears with a caress.

As they stood, a lady passerby stared with a disapproving look at their public display of emotion and affection. Char now began bawling.

"Oh, my dear sweet Char," Brady comforted her. "It will be all right."

But she shook her head.

"I know this is a terrible time for you," he said. "Losing someone you so admired and loved."

A moment of silence followed.

"It's not just that, Brady." She stared blankly down at her shoes.

"What?" His mouth fell open.

"I don't know if I want to talk about it now." The words eked out as she drew slightly away.

"What? Pl-please, Char. T-tell me," he stammered.

She turned toward him. "No, some other time. OK?"

"Char, you've opened this up. You need to get it all out."

"Who are we kidding, Brady?" she blurted out, her chin trembling. "Have you ever really thought about it?"

"What do you mean?" He reached for her hand, but she held hers tight.

"The two of us."

"I adore you. I always hoped our relationship would grow into something much more—blossom into something special."

"That's sweet, but face it, it would never work. Society just isn't ready for us. We both saw the look we just got from that stranger. A white boy with a mixed-race girl? We get those disapproving stares all the time. The two of us together is just out of place. I hate to say it, but it's like a printing press in the river. I'm sorry, Brady, but after some thought, I believe it comes down to friends—friends it must remain. That will have to be the extent of our relationship."

The door to the funeral director's home opened. Celia Ann, her eyes puffy and red, was followed out by Elijah's two brothers, their faces ashen, their shoulders slumping.

"The funeral will be tomorrow after all," she said. Turning to Charlotte, she queried, "I have a big favor to ask of you. Would you be able to stay home with little Edward? He loves having you over, and my dear sister needs to go to the funeral."

"Yes, that's fine. As much as I'd love to be at the funeral, I understand. I love little Edward—he's so much like his father. I'll watch after him." She sighed. "Does he know about his father yet?"

"No, not yet. I'm praying for the strength to tell him his daddy won't be coming home anymore." She put a hand on Charlotte's shoulder. "Thank you, Charlotte, you've always been there for us."

On Elijah Parish Lovejoy's thirty-fifth birthday, the day that would also be his burial day, church bells rang through the cold and rainy air. Other than family and close friends, few dared attend for fear of further mob unrest.

He was buried in a field near his home, with the ceremony comprising nothing more than a short prayer of blessing by Rev. Lippincott. There was no formal service, not even any flowers. Brady noticed an old Negro man standing at the back of the small group of mourners. He had been the gravedigger. Afterward, Brady found out he had refused any money for his services.

Chapter 23

In the following days, hundreds of newspapers across the country decried the horrible tragedy that had taken place in Alton, which now took on the reputation of a lawless town. Although leaders of the mob action were identified, including a few prominent doctors, no one was ever found guilty.

The abolitionist movement across the country gained significant new strength. Elijah's brother, Owen, admitted to Brady that Elijah's death probably helped the cause even more than if he had lived.

In Springfield, Illinois, State Representative Abraham Lincoln said, "Let every man remember that to violate the law is to trample on the blood of his father, and to tear the charter of his own and his children's liberty."

Other abolitionists from across the country helped to write for the Observer, which was printed elsewhere. But after several months, the newspaper was forced to shut down. Other publications carried the torch forward.

* * * * *

March 1838 (five months later in St. Louis)

Brady held his hands over his head to shield from the rain. He increased his gait as he ran for the sheltering veranda over the walkway before Smith's general store. He stopped to admire the newly mounted sign outside—Charlotte Jones, Seamstress. Feelings of pride rose up to buoy a heart still heavy with thoughts of good times gone.

He stepped through the door while smoothing his damp hair and nodded toward a lady customer on her way out. Ignoring the other customers, he ambled past a pickle barrel and shelves teeming with textiles on his way to Charlotte's work desk in the far corner.

"Good morning, Charlotte. Glad to see you're finally situated here in St. Louis." He took a step back in admiration. "Looks good."

She finished a stich and looked up. "Hello there, Brady. Yes, I'm so grateful to Mr. Smith for carving out some space for me. Of course, it all started over at Mr. Lovejoy's place. He got me this machine and helped me establish some customers there."

"How's that contraption working out for you?" He tilted his head to the side.

"Finally starting to get comfortable with it. No doubt, it does speed up my work. I think Mrs. Dithers is still mad at me. I've taken away some of her customers. But on the other hand, those people are happy because I'm able to charge them less." She demonstrated a few stiches on the machine, which responded with a rhythmic whir. "I love that sound," she said with a smile.

"So, what have you been doing in your spare time?" He braced a hip against the table and folded his arms across his chest, enjoying the sparkle in her big eyes.

"Besides sewing, I've been trying to write a poem."

"Poetry?" The word seemed to jolt him upright. "Wow, you've really come a long way, Char."

"It's not very good. I just wanted to express something about the loss of all those presses in the river and what the future might hold. But with Elijah's death, the future hasn't started out too good."

"Guess it all depends on how far into the future you look."

An extended silence followed until Charlotte changed the subject. "Oh, do you remember Malcolm—the one who made me that saddle?"

"Yes, how could I forget?" Visions of riding with Charlotte behind him sitting in her new saddle flashed into his mind. But it was her endearing arms clutching from behind that he remembered more than the saddle. He also could not forget Malcolm's brother Samuel's smile with his chipped tooth—how he was so determined to gain his freedom.

"Malcolm and I have been having a lot of fun together." She hummed along with the whir of the sewing machine.

"I see," Brady mumbled. Both remained quiet for a bit.

"So, what are you up to today?" she finally asked.

"I've got to get back up to Alton to clean out the printing office. But as far as I know, there's no new tenant anxious to get the space."

"What's left to do?" She placed a finished garment to the side with a gentle pat.

"Today I was going to tackle Mr. Lovejoy's desk. I've been putting that off—too emotional." He stared down at his fingernails.

"Understood." Charlotte's eyes locked on his. "God be with you then."

Brady turned to head out. He was happy for Charlotte, but that feeling soon turned a bit sour. What once was a budding romance was now just mere friendship. And Malcolm was his replacement. In the end, though, he must wish them both well.

* * * * *

Brady sat at Elijah's desk, pulling the drawers open, then closing them shut. Not until several minutes passed sitting in his chair was he able to linger with the thought of their contents. Inside were stacks of written sheets showing changes and edits—must have been the ones Elijah most admired. Thumbing through them, Brady noticed some with changes that were his ideas. Why couldn't he rejoice in the contributions he had made? After all, Elijah must have kept them for some reason.

No, not today! He must empty the drawers. He piled stack after stack of papers atop the desk.

But the bottom drawer on the right-hand side was different. Inside, he found strictly personal letters—mostly from Elijah's parents back East. He'd have to box them up for shipping to Celia Ann, who had moved back to St. Charles with her parents. As he pulled out each envelope and deposited it into a box, he couldn't help but admire how much they corresponded. How he needed to do a better job with his own father.

At the very bottom of the drawer was a different letter. It had been forwarded from the former St. Louis office of the Times. The return address was from a William Wells Brown in Cleveland, Ohio. Wait! Could it be that Sandford person he had chased years ago?

September 23rd

Dear Mr. Lovejoy,
I just wanted to write to let you know I am a free man now living in Cleveland, Ohio.

Two men have stood out in my life and will forever hold a special place in my heart. One is a Quaker who took me in when I was a fugitive slave and so desperate in Ohio. When I was hungry, he fed me and gave me shelter. He was my springboard to freedom. Running into him was truly serendipitous (hope you like that fancy word). I should rather say it was all God-ordained.

The other man most dear to my heart is you. One of the best times in my life was working for you as an apprentice. More than anyone, you helped me to learn to read and write. Your gift of *Robinson Crusoe* was much cherished. (Unfortunately, I lost it in a terrible catastrophe.)

Anyway, I just wanted to let you know how much you meant to me. If you are ever in the Cleveland area, please look me up. I'm a steward on the Detroit.

In loving admiration,

William Wells (Sandford) Brown

Brady dropped the letter and dashed out the door. At his uncle's place, he announced to his aunt he'd be making plans for a trip to Cleveland. He rocked on his heels, tilted his head back, and closed his eyes—another journey via steamboat! He thought about the long trip up the Ohio River, then the trek by land to Cleveland on the shores of Lake Erie.

Justice may have been a long time coming, but it must be served. He would be sure to pack his Bible, and his gun.

Chapter 24

On the Ohio River, Brady leaned over the railing of the Emperor and breathed in deeply to fill his senses. The trees passing by along the shoreline now displayed the fresh bright green of new leaves. The churning waters slapped by the paddlewheel created a reassuring sound. Yet a tingle continued to shoot up and down his spine. Was it from the chill of the April air, or was it from the unsettled thoughts filling his head? For sure, a battle was taking place in his mind.

Why am I still obsessed with confronting this William fellow? After all these years? William made a critical mistake, but haven't we all at some point? To think it all started with my throwing snowballs at him as a young kid. Why can't I just let it all go? Maybe, maybe it's because I loved my mother so much. But that was because she loved me first. Yes! I owe it to her. Absolutely! A fish jumped from the water in front of him.

But what would she want me to do now? What about Mr. Lovejoy? What would he advise? And God?

* * * * *

Now in Cleveland midmorning two days hence, he gazed out at Lake Erie's calm cold waters and watched for an inconspicuous moment to sneak on board the steamboat Detroit docked at the wharf. Where would the steward named William, alias Sandford, be at this time of day? The galley?

Managing to board unnoticed, Brady used his familiarity with steamboats to find the galley. There, a black man dressed in black pants and vest stood at a counter, his back to Brady. The unfor-gettable body shape and sideburns of the man appeared to be the same as Brady had seen on the Chester years ago.

"I'm sure you'd rather be here on the Detroit than on the Tecumseh," came Brady's opening snide remark. "Isn't that right, William? Or should I call you Sandford?" He crossed his arms, his shoulders back.

The man set down a pitcher and rotated, his eyes scanning Brady, then focusing on Brady's eyes.

"How is it you know me?" he asked with a tightened jaw.

"I'm Brady Scott. You blew me and my parents off the Tecumseh that fateful day five years ago. Seventeen people died, not the least of which was my mother." Brady clenched his fists. Visions of shrieking people and the body of his mother lying on the cold basement floor of the church raced into his mind. He reached inside his vest to find his gun. He needed the reassur-ance of the hard barrel of the pistol.

"That was a terrible day." William's chin trembled slightly as he looked away. "I'll never forget it."

"Of course, neither will I. The day you and your boys just kept stoking that fire—just kept shoving wood in till the boiler said enough and exploded." He shook his head.

"It was a foolish mistake on my part," William uttered softly. "I'm so sorry your mother was one of the casualties. If I could somehow change things, I would." He lifted an eyebrow and stared ahead blankly. "It has haunted me, and I've prayed about it every day. Believe me." He leaned in.

"Don't you think I've prayed about it too?" Brady blurted. "I've been ravaged with thoughts of revenge. I lost my mother, but on top of that, I lost my chance for my dream job." Brady's eyes searched the floor as he released a heavy sigh. "I was taking my final test to become a cub pilot." The words escaped almost of their own, soft and free. "Ever since, it's been like my name went down with the Tecumseh."

"I'm sorry—I really am." William's shoulders slouched.

Just then the door opened, and a young black boy darted in, dashed to William, and clutched his leg.

"I thought you were going to get us some food, weren't you?" The scowl on his face must have matched the hunger in his stomach.

"I am busy right now. In a little bit," William responded. He bent over and cupped his hands around the boy's face, then kissed the top of his head. "You'll have to be patient," he said as the tender tips of his fingers wiped the young man's brow. The boy turned and ran back out the door.

"Your son?" Brady asked.

"Oh, no, just a friend."

Brady's lips parted in an extended moment of breathless silence. Finally he interjected, "I suppose you've heard Mr. Lovejoy was killed last November."

"Yes, I do read the newspapers, you know. I loved the man. Did you work with him?" His eyes went glassy.

"Yes, and I am aware you did too—even before me." Brady took a stride to the side.

"Now there was a man who truly heard freedom's call." Tears now flowed freely down William's cheeks.

"So now I'm looking straight at a free man. Is that right? Did you purchase your freedom?"

"No sir. Nothing to purchase. Yes, it helps to be in free territory. But I've had my freedom all along. God gave it to me," he asserted, his jaw firm.

Absolutely no doubt about that, Brady thought. He was an equal in God's eyes. *What's more, this man is a warm, compassionate, and remorseful fellow—maybe more human than me. To think I once hunted him down like an animal! He certainly doesn't deserve to see the cold hard steel in my pocket!* Words from Scripture reverberated in his mind.

Brady took a few steps to the side, looking down, then turned back. "It's . . . taken a long time, William, but God has been pushing me to a new place with this whole mess. He keeps pushing, so maybe it's about time I listened."

"How's that?" William's lips parted slightly.

"It's become clearer to me, for sure. And I can't forget that on that day I was the one who got us into trouble in the first place. What's more, I was just as capable as you of making the same mistake stoking the furnace. We're all human. God has forgiven you."

William gazed downward and mouthed softly, "Yes, I feel that he has." Then he looked up, his eyes locking on Brady's as he asked, "But have you?"

Silence seized the moment.

"I . . . do forgive you," Brady responded, then swallowed hard. "I am sorry, William." Brady stared into his former nemesis's eyes, still wet with a brow that twitched.

He advanced a footstep forward, then stopped. "May I give a free man a hug?" he asked. A shiver rose through him.

William met him, and the two shared an extended embrace. Brady sniffled as his eyes teared up.

"Are you all right?" William asked, pulling back a step as they stood looking into each other's eyes, still close.

"You don't have the whole story, William." Brady paused to gather strength. "I'm sure that over the years life has been a hundred times more difficult for you than for me. But the worst part was I . . . " He sighed, then continued, "I actually paid money to have you hunted down. I feel so ashamed."

"Oh!" William blurted out. Brady could see the man's eyes going back to those dreadful events. "Wow," William continued. "That chase was quite the ordeal. Phew!" He took another stride to the side and twirled away, shaking his head. After a few moments of silence, he began again, "But, you know, that's all history. Let's put it behind us. You have forgiven me, so how can I not forgive you?" William's gaze lowered as he appeared to search for a change of subject.

Another man in natty sailor attire entered the galley.

"Why, here is Pilot Quigley," exclaimed William with a sigh of relief.

"Who do we have here?" the man asked, looking at Brady.

"Well . . . this is, er, a friend going way back to my Mississippi River days. Brady Scott's his name. Man, does he know that river!" came his upturned voice. "Better than all the hawks flying above it and all the fish swimmin' in it! Lots of piloting experience."

"Good to meet you," Brady said, extending his hand, but his emotional exhaustion caused him to struggle to muster the strength for a firm handshake.

The pilot held up a bag in his other hand.

"I stopped at Claire's Bakery this morning and saved a roll for you, William. Now maybe the two of you could split it."

"No, thank you," came back from both, almost in unison. "Appreciate the thought, though," William added.

"So, tell me, Brady," Pilot Quigley continued. "What brings you here?"

Silence followed.

"Well, er, since you've asked . . . " Brady stumbled with his words.

"He's checking on that opening for a cub pilot," William was quick to add.

Brady's head jerked up as he felt his eyes widening.

William smiled with a wink.

"Terrific," Mr. Quigley replied. "I've been looking for someone for quite a while now. These would be new waters for you though, right?"

"New, indeed. I like new challenges, though." Brady flashed a confident grin.

"As one of the big lakes, Erie is naturally one of the shallowest. Sometimes it gets pretty rough. You have to pay attention," the pilot said.

"But I'm sure it could be mastered in a short time," Brady replied.

"Well, then. Let me show you around the boat. Let's start at the top—the pilothouse. That's my favorite spot."

"Mine too!" Brady bounced from foot to foot like a kid.

His pulse raced as the pilot showed him one feature of the stately steamboat after another.

They ended up on the lower level where several skids of freight were stored. Brady happened to look behind a crate where a black man and woman cowered.

"Are they deckhands?" he asked.

"Oh no. Look a little farther behind the crate."

A young boy with big eyes peeked out—he was the same one who had come into the galley earlier.

"I'm not supposed to know they're here," Pilot Quigley whispered, his eyes gleaming as he turned toward the boy. "But since I've run into you, young man, I have one last sweet roll here in the bag, if you'd like it." The boy cast a pleading look toward his mother, who responded affirmatively.

Brady smiled down at the young man who soon had devoured a large bite of his roll. The way the boy's tongue licked lingering sugar off his lips reminded him of Mr. Lovejoy.

"Every trip, William brings two or three along," the pilot continued. "When we get to Canada, they step off the boat to a life of freedom."

Brady's heart pounded, and he tingled all over. He lifted his head and took in a large breath. But was the air as sweet as that of the Mississippi River? He spun decisively to Pilot Quigley.

"If you'll have me, sir, I'd love to be your cub pilot on the Detroit."

They shook hands again, Brady's grip now firmer than ever. *After all*, he thought, *this could be even sweeter!*

The End

Author Notes and Brief Biographies

This story represents what I call historical character fiction. Unlike other general historical fiction that places fictional characters in a specific timeframe, with perhaps a cameo appearance by a noted historical figure, the intent of this piece is to substantially reveal the noted character with personality and virtues. Hence, it is much closer to a biography.

In the course of crafting the story, however, certain specifics around happenings, dates, and exact order of events may be sacrificed. The challenge is to weave the events of a story as closely as possible to what actually happened in the significant person's life, per the biographies. In effect, then, this book is based on a true story, or as is the case here, on true stories.

I submit that it is far more likely a person will want to learn about a unique person of the past through story rather than by reading a biography. Reading the latter may hopefully follow, once the reader is intrigued by the historical figure's character who's been revealed in the story.

William Wells Brown

The son of a white man and slave woman, William Wells Brown was born in 1814 in Lexington, Kentucky, on a plantation owned by Dr. John Young. He spent his early years in a variety of jobs, including field hand, house servant, and tavern-keeper's helper in the St. Louis area. For a short time, he also worked as a printer's apprentice for Elijah Lovejoy. The account in Chapter

1 of the snowball incident comes substantially from Brown's autobiography, *Narrative of William Wells Brown, A Fugitive Slave*.

While a young boy, William was renamed Sandford, much to his chagrin, to avoid confusion with another William taken into the family.

As an eighteen-year-old, William was hired out to a slave trader, James Walker. He made several trips to New Orleans helping Walker manage and prepare his slaves for sale. During this time, he tried to escape to freedom with his mother, but they were both apprehended, then separated for good—a very traumatic event for the son.

William was later sold to Enoch Price, a riverboat owner and captain, who used him as a steamboat steward. Later in life (1848), William was offered his freedom by Price for $325.00. William replied that it was not possible because God already "made me free, as he did Enoch Price." He would not pay one penny.

In Cincinnati, on January 1, 1834, William took the opportunity to seize his freedom again. For six days, he wandered as a fugitive slave. He finally encountered a Quaker, Wells Brown, who provided temporary food and shelter. Not knowing his real last name, William took on the surname offered to him by the kind Quaker.

A free man, William eventually made it to Cleveland where he worked as a steward on a Lake Erie steamboat. He was active in helping other fugitive slaves escape to freedom in Canada. He also took on temperance issues.

Brown moved to Buffalo, married, and had two daughters. While there, his home became a stop on the Underground Railroad.

In later years, he gained success writing several books as well as lecturing against slavery, both in the US and abroad. In addition to his autobiography, other writings include *The Black Man: His Antecedents, His Genius, and His Achievements*; *My Southern*

Home; and *Clotel*, considered by many the first African American novel.

William Wells Brown died in 1884 at the age of seventy.

Other tidbits: Brown was never involved in a steamboat explosion. He presumably read *Robinson Crusoe* as he made reference to it in his writings. He was not actually hunted down by bloodhounds, but he does describe that prospect happening to others in writings elsewhere. He also described an incident involving a farm owner who nailed his barn shut to protect a fugitive slave.

Elijah P. Lovejoy

Elijah P. Lovejoy was born on a farm in 1802 in Maine, son of a preacher and the first of nine children. Education was stressed early in his family, and he went on to graduate from what is now called Colby College.

After early struggles with teaching and newspaper subscription sales, he received financial backing from the college president to head west to St. Louis where he established new roots. He became a partner and editor of the *St. Louis Times*.

During that time, he gravitated to the concept of colonization, the resettlement of American blacks in Africa, as a potential solution to slavery. While an editor, he hired a young black man, William Wells Brown, who went on to become a noted writer and abolition advocate as described above.

Lovejoy struggled to find his faith calling, eventually choosing to return to the East Coast to the Princeton Theological Seminary, after which he became a Presbyterian minister. Meanwhile, friends back in St. Louis saw a need for a morals and faith-based newspaper there. They offered financing for him to establish the *St. Louis Observer* in November 1833.

As an editor, Lovejoy did not shy away from controversial issues. He attacked liquor and tobacco use and even went as far as to confront the Catholic Church. When he eventually took a strong stance against slavery and for abolition on religious grounds, significant unrest was unleashed in the mostly pro-slavery community.

Lovejoy was forced to move to the free state of Illinois, setting up a new printing operation just across the Mississippi River in Alton in 1836, calling it the *Alton Observer*.

Opposition, however, did not wane, and mobs showed their displeasure by seizing his printing presses on multiple occasions, usually depositing them in the river. Lovejoy would not be deterred and continued to maintain his strong opposition to slavery.

Lovejoy called for a convention to be held in Alton to discuss the formation of a state anti-slavery society. At that congress, all points of view were welcome.

Meanwhile, a fourth printing press was on its way. Upon arrival, it was to be stored for safekeeping on the third floor of a warehouse.

On the night of November 7, 1837, an unruly mob gathered outside the warehouse. An attempt was made with a ladder to set fire to the wooden roof. Shots were exchanged. While trying to knock the ladder over, Lovejoy was shot several times and died immediately. No one was ever convicted for his murder.

Elijah P. Lovejoy was buried with no formal ceremony, as it was feared there might be further disruption. The service took place on what would have been his thirty-fifth birthday. Sixty years later, a monument to him was erected in Alton, Illinois.

Lovejoy's death became a rallying cry for abolitionists across the country. His pleas before his death defending his right to publish his views made him a champion of freedom of the press—a reputation that has lasted to this day.

Abraham Lincoln, a twenty-eight-year-old state representative from Illinois, decried the dangers of mob rule after Elijah's killing. Owen Lovejoy, Elijah's younger brother, went on to serve in the US Congress and became a strong voice for abolition. Later, President Lincoln called Owen Lovejoy the best friend he had in Congress and asked him to attend the signing of the Emancipation Proclamation in 1863.

Cave-in-Rock

Near the southern tip of Illinois, Cave-in-Rock has a storied history. Both a state park and small town now bear its name. A fifty-foot circumference opening marks this natural cave on a bluff overlooking the Ohio River.

Stories abound from the early 1800s of gangs of thieves and pirates with notorious leaders using the cave as a home base for their illicit activities. Unsuspecting travelers along the Ohio River were their primary victims. Crimes ranged from thefts and extortion to even suspected killings. Discovery nearby of buried tooling and dies seems to validate claims that counterfeiting was one of the many byproducts of that place and time in history.

Robinson Crusoe

One of the most highly renowned novels of all time, *Robinson Crusoe* was first published by Daniel Defoe in 1719. It depicts the 1650s life of an adventure-seeking Englishman who ends up shipwrecked on a tropical desert island. Carving out a mostly solitary life of introspection, Crusoe eventually connects with a slave named Friday, whom he saves from cannibals. Crusoe teaches Friday English and about Christianity. The two island-dwellers highly respect and love each other; however, Crusoe is clearly the "master."

Sewing Machine

In 1832, the first lockstitch sewing machine was invented by Water Hunt. He neglected to patent it, however, until 1854.

Boat Names

Many of the boats referenced in the story were actual river-boats of the time, although dates may not align. The Tecumseh was a wooden-hulled sidewheeler built in 1826 in Cincinnati. It was 174 feet long with 6 boilers, a gentlemen's cabin forward, and ladies' cabin aft. A boiler did not, however, explode as per the story.

Bibliography

Andrews, William L. *From Fugitive Slave to Free Man: The Autobiographies of William Wells Brown.* Columbia: University of Missouri, 2013.

Gillespie, Michael. *Come Hell or High Water: A Lively History of Steamboating on the Mississippi and Ohio Rivers.* Stoddard: Great River Publishing, 2001.

Simon, Paul. *Freedom's Champion: Elijah Lovejoy.* Carbondale: Southern Illinois University Press, 1994.

Twain, Mark. *Life on the Mississippi.* Chicago: Dover Publications, 2000.

About the Author

Doug is retired from business careers at Target, Amex, and 3M. He has been married over forty-three years to Leslie, and they have two children, Brian and Cristina, as well as grandchildren, Carissa, Luke, and Gabriella. Except for two short years teaching in Alabama, Doug is a lifelong resident of the Twin Cities, where winters are far more tolerable than common folklore dictates. His love of writing historical fiction came late in life—no doubt from creative urges fostered early by his inventive father, and now unbound from the shackles of the business world.

As a youngster he was a slow reader (OK, still is). So unlike many other authors, Doug can't say he devoured books (barbeque, yes). Although books with heavy description and literary flourish are appreciated, he gravitates to story. A fast-paced tale with strong characters revealing a loving and gracious God triumphs any day. If one can learn a bit of history along the way, so much the better. Hence, with his own writing, Doug tries to provide quick reads with meaningful glimpses of times past— stories of faith and life that transcend their historical timelines. Hopefully they will linger in minds longer than the time it takes to read them, as therein lies success.

A graduate of Cornell University, Doug currently serves on the Board of the Minnesota Inventors Hall of Fame, and when not writing, may be found in middle-school classrooms, inspiring kids to become inventors, or speaking on behalf of Feed My Starving Children.

Two of Doug's previous books are award-winners:

- 2018 Illuminate—Juvenile/YA Fiction Silver Award for *The Baker's Daughter: Braving Evil in WWII Berlin* (LPC Publishing).
- 2017 Moonbeam Children's—YA Fiction-Religion Silver Award for *Da Vinci's Disciples*.

Printed in the United States
By Bookmasters